A trip to the salt flats turns into a footrace!

Henry and Anna raced across the flats while all the visitors watched. The sun glared off the salt, and Henry's legs began to ache. Anna was running right toward the edge of the flat. He watched her silhouette, hoping that any moment she would start to slow down so he could gain on her. Suddenly, Anna's form disappeared. Henry frowned and ran onward. Then he tried to skid to a halt—but it was too late. He tripped on a mound of salt, almost invisible in the white daylight, and went tumbling over the other side...

THE BOXCAR CHILDREN MYSTERIES

THE BOXCAR CHILDREN
SURPRISE ISLAND
THE YELLOW HOUSE MYSTERY
MYSTERY RANCH
MIKE'S MYSTERY
BLUE BAY MYSTERY
THE WOODSHED MYSTERY
THE LIGHTHOUSE MYSTERY
MOUNTAIN TOP MYSTERY
SCHOOLHOUSE MYSTERY
CABOOSE MYSTERY
HOUSEBOAT MYSTERY
SNOWBOUND MYSTERY
TREE HOUSE MYSTERY
BICYCLE MYSTERY
MYSTERY IN THE SAND
MYSTERY BEHIND THE WALL
BUS STATION MYSTERY
BENNY UNCOVERS A MYSTERY
THE HAUNTED CABIN MYSTERY
THE DESERTED LIBRARY MYSTERY
THE ANIMAL SHELTER MYSTERY
THE OLD MOTEL MYSTERY
THE MYSTERY OF THE HIDDEN PAINTING
THE AMUSEMENT PARK MYSTERY
THE MYSTERY OF THE MIXED-UP ZOO
THE CAMP-OUT MYSTERY
THE MYSTERY GIRL
THE MYSTERY CRUISE
THE DISAPPEARING FRIEND MYSTERY
THE MYSTERY OF THE SINGING GHOST
THE MYSTERY IN THE SNOW
THE PIZZA MYSTERY
THE MYSTERY HORSE
THE MYSTERY AT THE DOG SHOW
THE CASTLE MYSTERY
THE MYSTERY OF THE LOST VILLAGE
THE MYSTERY ON THE ICE
THE MYSTERY OF THE PURPLE POOL
THE GHOST SHIP MYSTERY
THE MYSTERY IN WASHINGTON, DC
THE CANOE TRIP MYSTERY
THE MYSTERY OF THE HIDDEN BEACH
THE MYSTERY OF THE MISSING CAT
THE MYSTERY AT SNOWFLAKE INN

THE MYSTERY ON STAGE
THE DINOSAUR MYSTERY
THE MYSTERY OF THE STOLEN MUSIC
THE MYSTERY AT THE BALL PARK
THE CHOCOLATE SUNDAE MYSTERY
THE MYSTERY OF THE HOT AIR BALLOON
THE MYSTERY BOOKSTORE
THE PILGRIM VILLAGE MYSTERY
THE MYSTERY OF THE STOLEN BOXCAR
THE MYSTERY IN THE CAVE
THE MYSTERY ON THE TRAIN
THE MYSTERY AT THE FAIR
THE MYSTERY OF THE LOST MINE
THE GUIDE DOG MYSTERY
THE HURRICANE MYSTERY
THE PET SHOP MYSTERY
THE MYSTERY OF THE SECRET MESSAGE
THE FIREHOUSE MYSTERY
THE MYSTERY IN SAN FRANCISCO
THE NIAGARA FALLS MYSTERY
THE MYSTERY AT THE ALAMO
THE OUTER SPACE MYSTERY
THE SOCCER MYSTERY
THE MYSTERY IN THE OLD ATTIC
THE GROWLING BEAR MYSTERY
THE MYSTERY OF THE LAKE MONSTER
THE MYSTERY AT PEACOCK HALL
THE WINDY CITY MYSTERY
THE BLACK PEARL MYSTERY
THE CEREAL BOX MYSTERY
THE PANTHER MYSTERY
THE MYSTERY OF THE QUEEN'S JEWELS
THE STOLEN SWORD MYSTERY
THE BASKETBALL MYSTERY
THE MOVIE STAR MYSTERY
THE MYSTERY OF THE PIRATE'S MAP
THE GHOST TOWN MYSTERY
THE MYSTERY OF THE BLACK RAVEN
THE MYSTERY IN THE MALL
THE MYSTERY IN NEW YORK
THE GYMNASTICS MYSTERY
THE POISON FROG MYSTERY
THE MYSTERY OF THE EMPTY SAFE
THE HOME RUN MYSTERY
THE GREAT BICYCLE RACE MYSTERY

THE MYSTERY OF THE WILD PONIES
THE MYSTERY IN THE COMPUTER GAME
THE HONEYBEE MYSTERY
THE MYSTERY AT THE CROOKED HOUSE
THE HOCKEY MYSTERY
THE MYSTERY OF THE MIDNIGHT DOG
THE MYSTERY OF THE SCREECH OWL
THE SUMMER CAMP MYSTERY
THE COPYCAT MYSTERY
THE HAUNTED CLOCK TOWER MYSTERY
THE MYSTERY OF THE TIGER'S EYE
THE DISAPPEARING STAIRCASE MYSTERY
THE MYSTERY ON BLIZZARD MOUNTAIN
THE MYSTERY OF THE SPIDER'S CLUE
THE CANDY FACTORY MYSTERY
THE MYSTERY OF THE MUMMY'S CURSE
THE MYSTERY OF THE STAR RUBY
THE STUFFED BEAR MYSTERY
THE MYSTERY OF ALLIGATOR SWAMP
THE MYSTERY AT SKELETON POINT
THE TATTLETALE MYSTERY
THE COMIC BOOK MYSTERY
THE GREAT SHARK MYSTERY
THE ICE CREAM MYSTERY
THE MIDNIGHT MYSTERY
THE MYSTERY IN THE FORTUNE COOKIE
THE BLACK WIDOW SPIDER MYSTERY
THE RADIO MYSTERY
THE MYSTERY OF THE RUNAWAY GHOST
THE FINDERS KEEPERS MYSTERY
THE MYSTERY OF THE HAUNTED BOXCAR
THE CLUE IN THE CORN MAZE
THE GHOST OF THE CHATTERING BONES
THE SWORD OF THE SILVER KNIGHT
THE GAME STORE MYSTERY
THE MYSTERY OF THE ORPHAN TRAIN
THE VANISHING PASSENGER
THE GIANT YO-YO MYSTERY
THE CREATURE IN OGOPOGO LAKE
THE ROCK 'N' ROLL MYSTERY
THE SECRET OF THE MASK
THE SEATTLE PUZZLE
THE GHOST IN THE FIRST ROW
THE BOX THAT WATCH FOUND
A HORSE NAMED DRAGON

THE GREAT DETECTIVE RACE
THE GHOST AT THE DRIVE-IN MOVIE
THE MYSTERY OF THE TRAVELING TOMATOES
THE SPY GAME
THE DOG-GONE MYSTERY
THE VAMPIRE MYSTERY
SUPERSTAR WATCH
THE SPY IN THE BLEACHERS
THE AMAZING MYSTERY SHOW
THE PUMPKIN HEAD MYSTERY
THE CUPCAKE CAPER
THE CLUE IN THE RECYCLING BIN
MONKEY TROUBLE
THE ZOMBIE PROJECT
THE GREAT TURKEY HEIST
THE GARDEN THIEF
THE BOARDWALK MYSTERY
THE MYSTERY OF THE FALLEN TREASURE
THE RETURN OF THE GRAVEYARD GHOST
THE MYSTERY OF THE STOLEN SNOWBOARD
THE MYSTERY OF THE WILD WEST BANDIT
THE MYSTERY OF THE GRINNING GARGOYLE
THE MYSTERY OF THE SOCCER SNITCH
THE MYSTERY OF THE MISSING POP IDOL
THE MYSTERY OF THE STOLEN DINOSAUR BONES
THE MYSTERY AT THE CALGARY STAMPEDE
THE SLEEPY HOLLOW MYSTERY
THE LEGEND OF THE IRISH CASTLE
THE CELEBRITY CAT CAPER
HIDDEN IN THE HAUNTED SCHOOL
THE ELECTION DAY DILEMMA
JOURNEY ON A RUNAWAY TRAIN
THE CLUE IN THE PAPYRUS SCROLL
THE DETOUR OF THE ELEPHANTS
THE SHACKLETON SABOTAGE
THE KHIPU AND THE FINAL KEY

THE BOXCAR CHILDREN®

CREATED BY
GERTRUDE CHANDLER WARNER

GREAT
5
ADVENTURE

THE KHIPU AND THE FINAL KEY

STORY BY
DEE GARRETSON and **JM LEE**

ILLUSTRATED BY
ANTHONY VanARSDALE

ALBERT WHITMAN & COMPANY
CHICAGO, ILLINOIS

Contents

The City of Fair Winds

Henry, Jessie, Violet, and Benny sat in their hotel room and stared at a small glass jar. The label on the jar read *dulce de leche*, and the syrupy substance inside had the thickness and color of caramel. The hotel clock read almost midnight where they were in Christchurch, New Zealand. It was very late for the four of them, especially six-year-old Benny, who let out a big yawn. Normally they would all be in bed, but a recent discovery kept them all awake.

"I can't believe Mr. Ganert is a spy," said Violet, who was eight years old. "Just think. Our pilot! He's traveled to every stop with us and has been telling the Argents our every move. No wonder Anna Argent was able to find us."

1

"At least it was Mr. Ganert and not Emilio," said Benny, thinking of the second of their two pilots. "I like Emilio's jokes. If he was the spy, we wouldn't get to hear any more of them."

Henry, who was fourteen years old and the oldest, agreed.

"We should call Trudy," he said. "Jessie, will you get your laptop and see if you can reach her on Skype? Do you think she's awake?"

Jessie nodded and unzipped her backpack. She was twelve years old, and she was the best among her siblings at using the laptop. Her skills had come in handy many times during their recent worldwide travels.

"Hmm, let's see," Jessie said. "If it's midnight here, it'll be six o'clock in the morning in Connecticut. We might wake her up, but I think this is important."

Jessie opened Skype and clicked on Trudy Silverton's name. She crossed her fingers and clicked the green button to start the call.

"Let's just hope Trudy has some good advice," Jessie said. "We only have one artifact left, and we're not going to let Mr. Ganert get in the way of returning it."

Violet glanced at the hotel dresser. Sitting on top was a small, plastic box. It was safely locked, just like the other five had been. If the previous boxes were any clue, the last box would hold a precious artifact that had been lost. The Aldens had been sent by Trudy Silverton to return the boxes. She worked for a secret organization called the Reddimus Society—which made sense, because *reddimus* was Latin for "we return." So far, the Aldens had successfully returned six other artifacts. They had only one left, and the Aldens were determined to finish their task, even if one of their pilots was a spy.

"Hello, Jessie! Hello, Henry, Violet, and Benny!"

Trudy's cheerful voice was a welcome sound. The Aldens gathered around Jessie's laptop so they could all see her and wave hello. It was very early in the morning where Trudy was, and her purple hair was a little disheveled. She was still in her pajamas.

"Good morning!" Jessie said. "We're so glad you're awake. We have something important to tell you."

Even though Trudy looked tired, she seemed to be lively and alert.

"Do you?" she asked. "Very interesting. I wonder if it's related to the important thing I have to tell all of you. Why don't you go first."

Henry lowered his voice even though Mr. Ganert wasn't anywhere nearby.

"You remember back in Thailand when we found out one of our pilots was telling the Argents about our travels?" Henry asked.

"Yes, you were all very clever!" replied Trudy.

"We were clever again," Jessie said. "We found out which one of the pilots is the spy. Henry came up with a great plan while we were flying back to New Zealand from Antarctica. We—"

"It's Mr. Ganert!" Benny blurted. "Mr. Ganert's the spy!"

"I guess the explanation will have to be a story for another day." Henry chuckled.

"That's great!" Trudy said. Then she tilted her head. "Well, it's not great that he's a spy, but it's great that you figured it out. Now we know he can't be trusted."

"And it helps Tricia too, right?" Jessie asked. The children had recently learned that there was an investigation going on into thefts around the world. Because Tricia had been seen in the areas of thefts in Kenya, Italy, and Japan, the investigators thought she might be secretly working with the Argents. But now the Aldens could prove otherwise.

"Yes, I will let Agent Carter know," Trudy said. "We now have evidence showing it's Mr. Ganert who is working for the Argents, not Tricia. Tricia will be so relieved to hear the news, if I can ever get ahold of her."

"What are we going to do about Mr. Ganert?" Jessie asked. "Can you send another pilot to take his place? If he stays as our pilot, he could make trouble for us when we try to return the last box."

Trudy shook her head.

"I'm sorry. I can't. That brings me to the thing I have to tell all of you. I received a message last night about the final artifact. According to the message, it's important that the seventh artifact is delivered quickly and to the right place. Even if he is a spy, Mr. Ganert is the best pilot Reddimus has. That's why we sent him with you...So unfortunately, we don't have time to find another pilot as skilled as he is."

"Can we fly with one pilot?" Jessie asked.

"I'm afraid you'll need two pilots to make a trip of any real distance."

Henry sighed in frustration. "In order to return the box, we have to fly with a pilot who's trying to steal it! This won't be easy."

"No, it won't," Trudy agreed. "But you have outsmarted Mr. Ganert and Anna Argent up until now, and you didn't even know there was a spy traveling with you. I know you will be able to outsmart him one last time."

"He might be extra grumpy because this will be his last chance to steal a Reddimus artifact," Henry said. "What if he tries something desperate?"

"Desperate people make more mistakes than patient ones," Trudy said. "Remember that and focus on yourselves. Take your time making good decisions. If you do, I'm sure you will have the last artifact returned in no time, and then we will deal with Mr. Ganert."

They said their good-byes, and Jessie closed the laptop with a big yawn.

"We had better get some rest," she said.

"Yes," said Henry. "Tomorrow will be another big day."

"I hope we find out our next destination soon," Violet added. Jessie's sleepiness was contagious, and Violet yawned too.

Benny would have agreed, but he had already fallen asleep.

The next morning, the Aldens got ready for a day of travel. They had been traveling for so long that it had become habit to expect a plane ride on the Reddimus jet.

Benny was ready first, and he inspected the jar of dulce de leche while he waited for his brother and sisters. The liquid in the jar was thick like honey. It reminded Benny of the topping on Mrs. McGregor's caramel apple pie. His stomach growled.

"Jessie, can I please try some of the dulce de leche?" he asked. "The jar wasn't in the Reddimus box, so it's not the artifact we have to return. It should be okay to taste just a little bit, right?"

Jessie laughed. "You're right. The jar is probably a treat for us to try. But I don't want you to eat too much. It will spoil your appetite."

The lid was on tight, so Jessie helped Benny open it. They didn't have any spoons in the hotel room, so Benny just used his finger. The topping inside was thick enough to spread, but drippy enough that Benny had to put his finger in his mouth quickly to keep from making a mess. The dulce de leche was sweet and sticky, with a flavor like caramel and butterscotch.

"You know, this jar is probably our next clue," Jessie remarked. Henry and Violet were ready to go now too, and all four of them took turns tasting the delicious topping. "Aside from the tag that says 'Fair Winds,' we don't know anything else about it."

"Since it's a food, maybe we should ask a chef," Violet suggested. "Someone who knows a lot about food might be able to tell us something that will help us."

Henry thumbed his chin and nodded. "The hotel restaurant was pretty nice. I'll bet the chefs there know about this sort of thing. Let's start there. We could use some breakfast anyway!"

The Aldens left their room and went down to the hotel restaurant. The night before, the restaurant was where they had figured out which of their pilots was the spy. Now the restaurant had a more relaxed feel, with bright windows and quiet hotel visitors having their morning coffee. The Aldens got a table and ordered the New Zealander's breakfast that was pictured on the menu.

"Cereal and toast with juice!" Benny said. "Just like breakfast back home. We should let Mrs. McGregor and Grandfather know we've been eating like people from New Zealand this whole time!"

After breakfast, Henry asked the waiter if they could speak with a chef, and soon someone came out of the kitchen. He was a lean man with dark hair and a well-groomed mustache.

"Good morning! Is there a problem?" The man spoke with a Spanish accent.

"Oh no, not at all. The food is very good," Henry assured him. "We were just wondering if we could ask you some questions. We're trying to solve a riddle. Can you tell us anything about dulce de leche?"

Benny, who had been holding the jar, showed it to the chef. The chef looked over the jar with a twinkle in his eye.

"There is a lot to tell about dulce de leche," he said. "I'm not sure where to start. It's a dessert topping first used in my home country, Argentina. The name means 'candy of milk.' It's very popular! In fact, I'm using it for a dessert on our menu right now."

"Argentina?" asked Jessie.

"Dessert?" added Benny.

"Oh yes! My family is from Buenos Aires, Argentina. I came here to study cooking. Ah, this dulce de leche is a brand I remember from back home. It makes me miss being there."

"Argentina. That's in South America," said Violet.

"It's also the last continent we haven't visited," said Henry. "It makes sense that it would be our last destination."

"You need to figure out your destination using

this treat as a clue?" asked the chef. Now that he understood, he looked at the jar more closely.

"Yes, this was our only clue," said Henry. "Argentina is a great start. But still, it's a big country. We don't know where in Argentina we need to go."

"Ah, what's this?" asked the chef. He had noticed the little tag on the jar. "'Fair winds.' Oh, my heart. It really does remind me of home!"

"You know what that means?" asked Benny.

The chef smiled widely.

"Of course! In Spanish, *Buenos Aires* means 'fair winds.' Buenos Aires is the capital of Argentina. If I could send you one place in the country, that is the place I would send you. It's a lively, beautiful place."

The news was the best way to start the day. The Aldens exchanged glances of excitement and relief.

"You know what this means?" Henry asked.

"Buenos Aires!" Benny exclaimed. "We're going to Buenos Aires!"

CHAPTER 2

An Unexpected Arrival

The Aldens finished breakfast and took a shuttle to the airport, where they met Emilio and Mr. Ganert. The Reddimus jet was sleek and shiny, parked on a private runway. It gleamed in the morning sun.

"The jet must have gotten a bath while we were in Antarctica! It's so shimmery!" Violet said.

Both of the pilots were waiting on board. They stood at attention and listened eagerly as the Aldens revealed that their next destination was Buenos Aires.

"Great news!" said Emilio. "We were worried when the clue turned up and we didn't hear from you about the next stop."

Mr. Ganert was more grumpy than usual.

Normally he said one or two things when they announced their next journey, but today he didn't say a single word. Once he knew where they were going, he disappeared into the cockpit.

"He's been in a foul mood all morning," Emilio said when Mr. Ganert was gone. "I don't know what's gotten into him."

The jet rumbled to life as Mr. Ganert started up the engines. Henry glanced toward the cockpit door, which Mr. Ganert had closed behind him. Between the sound of the engines and the closed door, he was sure Mr. Ganert wouldn't be able to hear them. He motioned for Emilio to come closer. The four Aldens and Emilio huddled in the cabin of the jet and whispered.

"We found out last night that Mr. Ganert is an Argent spy," Henry told Emilio.

Emilio raised his eyebrows and started to smile, as if he thought it might be a joke, but when he saw the serious faces of the Alden children, his smile went away and he nodded.

"Those messages last night—you sent them, didn't you? It was part of a test, to see which of us is a spy. You children are very clever! I have to say, I was wondering why you seemed to be holding out on me for the past few days. I'm sorry that I gave you any cause for suspicion, but I'm glad you've figured out it was Mr. Ganert. That would explain why he's been acting so strangely...and why he's so grumpy now! You've found him out, and he knows it."

"We called Trudy and told her, but she said that it's urgent that we return the last Reddimus artifact right away," explained Jessie. "She said there's no time to find another pilot. So in the meantime, please help us do whatever we can to return the last artifact."

Emilio nodded.

"You can count on me," he assured them. "Now, I ought to go be a proper copilot. I'll make sure we fly to Buenos Aires at double-time, and I'll keep an eye on Mr. Ganert."

The Aldens took their seats as the jet taxied to the runway. In a few minutes, they were in the air, watching Christchurch grow smaller and smaller behind them.

"My tummy doesn't feel so good," Benny said.

"It's from all the dulce de leche you've been sneaking from the jar all morning!" Violet laughed.

"Oooof!" groaned Benny.

"Benny, why don't you try to take a nap," suggested Jessie. "We were up late last night. It would be good for us all to get some rest."

Henry stretched out on one chair he had converted into a small bed. Most airplane cabins were not large enough for the chairs to turn into beds, but the Reddimus Society had made sure the Aldens traveled comfortably. After all, they had seen six of the world's seven continents since they had left their home in Greenfield, Connecticut.

"When we reach Buenos Aires, we will have a lot to take care of," Henry said. "Even if Emilio can keep Mr. Ganert out of our hair, we're still going to need to figure out how to open the last Reddimus box and find out where we're taking whatever's inside."

"And return it!" said Benny.

"I'm surprised we haven't received the clue about how to open the next box yet," said Violet. "I hope we get it soon."

An Unexpected Arrival

The flight from New Zealand to Buenos Aires was a long one—almost fifteen hours cutting straight across the Southern Ocean. There wasn't much to look at out the windows except for endless ocean, so the Aldens napped and took turns reading about Argentina on Jessie's laptop.

Jessie had started studying Spanish in school, so she spent her turn on the Internet refreshing her memory. She looked up important phrases, like how to ask for directions and say "please" and "thank you." Buenos Aires was a big, busy city, and they would need to find their way safely on their own. Especially if they would be exploring without one of the pilots, the more Spanish Jessie remembered, the better.

Like New Zealand, Argentina was a country in the Southern Hemisphere. That meant while it was spring in back in Connecticut, it was fall in Argentina. Still, the day was warm and bright when the Aldens arrived. As the children got ready to leave the plane, they were surprised to see Mr. Ganert come out from the cockpit.

"I will accompany you this time," he said. "I've

never come out on your trips, and I've wanted to see Buenos Aires for some time."

The Aldens were quiet. They stood halfway down the steps that led from the jet to the tarmac. Even Henry didn't know what to say. He didn't want Mr. Ganert to come with them, but how could he say so without sounding rude?

Emilio hurried out, just in time.

"Oh, Mr. Ganert!" he exclaimed. "There's a light flashing in the cockpit that I don't understand. Could you come inside and help me figure it out?"

"A flashing light?" Mr. Ganert asked, arching a brow. "Just a moment, children. I'll be right back."

As Mr. Ganert went back into the jet, Emilio winked and waved at them. The Aldens nodded and hurried off. By the time Mr. Ganert came back to the stairway, they would be too far for him to catch up.

Whenever the Aldens had arrived somewhere on their journey, someone had always been waiting to meet them and help them check in with their passports. This time no one was waiting, so they would have to do it themselves. Henry took the lead. He had watched closely all the times before. He walked up to the airport security agent, making sure he had all their passports ready.

"Hello, welcome to Buenos Aires," said the attendant in English when he saw that the Aldens had US passports. "What is the intent of your visit, and how long will you be staying?"

"We're here on vacation and hoping to return an item that was left with us," explained Henry. "We're not planning to stay longer than a couple days."

The attendant nodded and looked through their passports and their tickets.

"Oh, I see you're flying with the Reddimus Society," he said. "Very good. Please enjoy your stay in Argentina!"

The attendant stamped their passports and waved them through. Henry returned everyone's passports and followed the signs to exit the bustling airport.

"The first thing we need to do is find a place to stay while we wait for the next clue," he said.

"All the other times, the hotels were booked and

ready for us when we landed," Benny said. "Do you think we'll be able to book a hotel on our own?"

"It is strange that no one was here to meet us," Jessie said. She squeezed Benny's hand. "But we were able to check in on our own. We've learned a lot about travel since we started this trip."

Benny nodded and squeezed back. Henry paused at the information desk near one of the airport exits. There were many grand hotels advertised there, and he took his time looking through them.

"We'll want one near the airport, but also, the artifact probably has something to do with history. So it'll be good if we're close to the city center, where all the museums are. At the very least, it'll make research easier if we need to look anything up."

"There are so many restaurants and sights to see!" Violet said, picking out one of the pamphlets and reading through it. She showed Benny the colorful photos of elegant tango dancers. "I think we'll have a fun time here!"

Just then, a man approached them, weaving his way through the crowd of travelers. He had an envelope, which he pushed into Jessie's hands before quickly disappearing into the crowd again.

"What just happened?" Henry asked. "Was that a messenger?"

Jessie flipped over the envelope. The flap was sealed with an owl sticker. The owl was the symbol of the Reddimus Society and a sign that the message was about the artifact they were trying to return.

"It has the Reddimus owl on it, but that was a weird way to deliver it," Jessie said.

"It is strange, but let's open it and see what it says," Henry suggested.

Jessie opened the envelope. Inside was a strip of paper with letters on it, but none of the words made any sense:

!YRRUH .SEDNARG SANILAS EHT OT RAC A TNER .ATLAS OT OG

Jessie passed it around so everyone had a chance to look.

"The exclamation point is at the start," Benny pointed out. "It should be at the end."

Benny's observation gave Violet an idea.

"Y-R-R-U-H is *HURRY* written backward," she said. She took out a pencil and handed it to Jessie. "Let's see if the whole thing is a message written backward."

Jessie took the pencil, and Violet read the letters to her in reverse order. A minute later, they had reordered all the letters. The new message read:

GO TO SALTA. RENT A CAR TO THE SALINAS GRANDES. HURRY!

"Rent a car?" Henry asked. "But none of us can drive!"

Jessie sighed. "What are we going to do? We could call a taxi, but we don't know what the Salinas Grandes is or how far it is from here. Not to mention the fact that we haven't exchanged our money yet, so we wouldn't be able to pay the driver!"

Benny's ears perked when a voice came over the airport speaker system. The voice had been making announcements in different languages the entire time they had been in the airport, but this time a message in English caught his attention.

"Will Henry, Jessie, Violet, and Benny please come to the information booth in Terminal A, Gate Two."

Benny pointed toward the ceiling to get everyone to listen. The message repeated once more.

"That's us!" he exclaimed, tugging Henry's sleeve. "Terminal A, Gate Two. Maybe it'll be someone to drive us to Salinas Grandes!"

"I hope so," Henry said as they started looking for Terminal A. "It's pretty hard for us to hurry without a way to get anywhere!"

The Khipu and the Final Key

The airport was not too big, and they found Gate Two in Terminal A by following the signs. Waiting at the information desk was a familiar man. Though he was nearly sixty years old, his dark brown hair didn't have a strand of gray. When the Aldens recognized him, they ran to greet him.

"Grandfather!" they all cried at once.

Grandfather hugged them all tightly.

"Henry, Jessie, Violet, Benny!" he exclaimed. "Hello there!"

"What are you doing here, Grandfather?" Benny asked.

"Trudy told me about what's been going on with Mr. Ganert and everything," Grandfather replied. "When you figured out you were going to Buenos Aires, Trudy and I thought it was a good idea for me to come and help you through your last Reddimus delivery."

"What about Watch? Is he with you?" Violet asked. The children had missed their dog while they were away too.

"No, I left him with Mrs. McGregor," Grandfather replied. "But he's doing just fine. He misses all four of you very much, but I told him he would see you very soon."

Grandfather looked them over, one by one, and noticed the piece of paper and envelope in Jessie's hand.

"I see you've already met someone from the Reddimus Society here," Grandfather said. "I'm glad to see they didn't have any trouble finding you."

"What do you mean?" Jessie asked.

"Trudy had told me you would be arriving at different gate," Grandfather said. "That's why I didn't meet you right away. It's also why I had them make an announcement over the speaker system!"

"Well, if the Argents were trying to keep us apart, they failed," Henry said. "Now we can get to where we need to go."

"I'm glad I can help," Grandfather said. "Where are we going?"

Jessie nodded and showed Grandfather the paper.

"The Salinas Grandes," she said. "Do you have any idea where or what it is?"

The Khipu and the Final Key

Grandfather stroked his chin in thought.

"Hmm, yes, I may. I heard a passenger on my flight mentioning it. It is a salt flat north of here. I heard she was meeting a flight here on her way to Salta. Let's see if we can catch the same flight!"

CHAPTER 3

The Great Salt Plain

Thanks to Grandfather, in a few minutes they all had new tickets. The flight was leaving soon, though, so they hurried to the gate. They arrived just in time to check in, and after only a few minutes, they were buckled in and on their way to Salta. The cabin was snug and cozy compared with the Reddimus jet or the big military plane they had taken to Antarctica.

"I like traveling on the Reddimus jet, but I like being around other people too," Benny said. He had the window seat and watched the clouds below them.

"Me too," agreed Jessie. She listened to the many passengers speaking Spanish. She could even make out some of the words.

The Khipu and the Final Key

Compared with the other flights they had taken, the trip to Salta was very short. In almost no time, they had landed again. The children waited while Grandfather spoke to a rental car manager. The manager didn't speak much English, and Grandfather didn't speak much Spanish, so Jessie helped out. Between the three of them, they were able to rent a car, but not before making a few mistakes that had them all laughing.

Grandfather got the car's GPS set up, and they began to drive toward the salt flats. The GPS estimated it was about three and a half hours, so they settled in to watch the Argentinian scenery. While they drove, Benny and Violet took turns telling Grandfather about all of their travels so far: riding camels and exploring the pyramids in Cairo, walking on a part of the Great Wall of China in Mutianyu, playing with dingoes and kangaroos in Australia, and peeking inside Ernest Shackleton's Antarctic exploration base. Grandfather listened eagerly.

"What a busy spring break you kids have had!" he said once they had finished.

"That reminds me," Jessie said. "With all the things we've been doing with the Reddimus Society, I almost forgot: spring break should actually be over."

Henry's eyes widened. "You're right! We should have been going back to school today."

"But helping the Reddimus Society is important too," Violet added.

"Don't worry about that," said Grandfather. "From the sound of it, you are learning all sorts of things on your travels. And I made sure to call your school before I left. There will be some makeup work when you get back, but your teachers are excited for you to travel."

"Phew!" said Benny. "We can do our makeup work in the boxcar! That will be fun."

"Thanks for taking care of that, Grandfather," said Jessie. "You're the best."

Grandfather chuckled and grinned. "You're just saying that because I'm the only one with a driver's license!"

The land surrounding the city of Salta was rocky and mountainous, with rivers running through red sand and rock, and green trees and bushes filling every pocket of earth. Soon the road began to twist and curve, going up into the mountains. Grandfather drove slowly so he could take the tight turns as they made their way higher and higher.

"It looks like a perfect day to visit the salt flats," Grandfather remarked as they neared their destination.

"Do you know how a salt flat gets made, Grandfather?" asked Violet.

"Good question, Violet," Grandfather answered. "Salt flats form when a lake dries up. In wet climates, lakes don't easily dry up. But in the desert, water evaporates quickly, and when it's gone, all that's left on the ground is the salt that was in the water."

The road straightened out, and everyone squinted against the bright afternoon sunlight. Ahead on the road was a huge field of white.

"Is that snow?" Benny asked.

"No, that's the salt!" Henry said. "Wow, it looks just like a big sheet of ice, though, doesn't it?"

"Almost like a piece of Antarctica right here in Argentina!" Violet said.

The Great Salt Plain

As they got closer, they started to see booths of artists and merchants selling salt sculptures, pottery, and handmade textiles. Grandfather parked the car and found a merchant selling sunglasses. The merchant's booth was busy because it was such a sunny day. Many people crowded around the little stand. Everyone bumped into each other and talked about how excited they were to explore the flats. When the Aldens were finally at the front of the line, Grandfather bought a pair for himself and for each of his grandchildren.

"Oh, that's much better," said Jessie, putting on the sunglasses.

"The salt is reflecting so much light!" Henry agreed. "That sunglasses seller has the right idea."

With the sunglasses on, they were finally able to look around. The salt flat was a huge stretch of land, entirely covered in pure-white salt. It stretched into the distance on all sides of the road. Some parts were smooth, and others were cracked and rippled from the sun. Under the clear blue sky, it was breathtaking.

"It really does look like snow," Violet said as they

walked out onto the salt. Benny reached down to touch it. The raw salt felt hard and light, like table salt. But the crystals were much bigger.

"Can we eat it?" Benny asked. "It's just salt, right?"

"You could, but someone might have walked on it already," Grandfather said with a wink. That didn't bother Benny. Who knew when he would have another chance to eat natural salt? He picked up a cluster and tasted it.

"So? How is it?" Jessie asked.

"Salty!" Benny said, and they all laughed.

Henry checked his watch. "I'm surprised we haven't heard from a Reddimus agent yet," he said.

Jessie frowned. "Do you think something's wrong?"

"I don't know," Henry said. "We already thought the last message delivery was strange. And there was the problem of meeting up with Grandpa at the airport. Then we spent all the time to come out here, but no one's come to find us..."

"Maybe we got tricked," Benny suggested. He didn't sound too disappointed. Even if they had been tricked, they still had gotten to visit Salinas Grandes and eat natural salt.

Violet sighed. "Mr. Ganert must have realized that we know he's the spy by now. He even tried to come out with us this morning. Do you think the messenger at the airport was a spy?"

"But the envelope had the owl sticker!" Benny said.

Jessie took the envelope out of her backpack and looked at it again.

"Yes, but Mr. Ganert has seen other Reddimus envelopes," she said. "It wouldn't be difficult for him to find an owl sticker and put it on there, just to make us think it was real."

"Plus, now that I look at it closer, the sticker doesn't look as neat as the ones we usually see on the envelopes," Violet said.

Henry looked down at his watch to check how long they had been waiting. When he did, he noticed the snap on his camera bag was dangling open. With his heart racing, Henry opened the case and looked inside.

"Oh no!" he cried. "The Reddimus box is gone!

When could this have happened?"

"It must have been while we were waiting to buy sunglasses!" Jessie said. "It was so bright we could hardly see anything, and there were so many people."

"Is Anna here?" Benny asked, looking around. Since buying sunglasses, most of the visitors had scattered and were wandering around and exploring. The five Aldens scanned the area. It was Violet who caught sight of a woman with a blond ponytail walking swiftly up the road to where the cars were parked. She was carrying something in one hand.

"There she is!" Violet said, pointing. "If she makes it to her car, she'll get away!"

The children broke into a sprint. It wasn't easy to run on the hard salt. Benny had shorter legs than everyone, and Violet slowed down so she wouldn't trip. Jessie and Henry kept running, but Jessie was carrying her laptop in her backpack.

"Don't worry, Jessie!" Henry said. "I'll get to her before she gets to her car!"

"Be careful!" Jessie called, slowing down and leaning on her knees.

Henry was a strong runner. In fact, that was how he had first met Grandfather, before he had known who his grandfather was. Once a year, Grandfather put on a free-for-all race, and one day Henry had decided to enter and had won. Now, as he ran against the clock to beat Anna Argent to her car and save the last Reddimus artifact, he remembered that day. Behind him, he heard Grandfather and his siblings cheering him on.

"Run, Henry!" they cried. "You can do it!"

"That's my boy!" Grandfather shouted.

The salt crackled and flew up under Henry's shoes as he dashed onward, racing to catch up with Anna Argent. When he got closer, she noticed him and started running. She looked between him and her red jeep and realized she wouldn't reach it before he would.

"Give back the Reddimus box!" Henry called to her.

"No!" Anna yelled back. And with that, she spun on her heel and started running in the other direction, onto the salt flats.

By now, everyone around had stopped to watch

the chase take place. Henry had already run what he thought was about a quarter-mile. He could easily run another three-quarters. But he wasn't sure whether he would catch up to Anna. She was a powerful runner. Early in the Aldens' journey, she had caught up with a moving train. In fact, Henry had never seen her without her sneakers on.

Henry and Anna raced across the flats while all the visitors watched. The sun glared off the salt, and Henry's legs began to ache. Anna was running right toward the edge of the flat. It seemed she hoped Henry would grow tired and give up so she could escape, but Henry was determined to catch up. He watched her silhouette against the bright salt, hoping that any moment she would start to slow down so he could gain on her.

Suddenly, Anna's form disappeared. Henry frowned and ran onward. Then he tried to skid to a halt—but it was too late. He tripped on a mound of salt, almost invisible in the white daylight, and went tumbling over the other side.

Henry groaned. His elbow was bruised, and he was all wet. He had landed in a shallow pool of water. The fall had left scrapes on Henry's knees and elbows, and the saltwater in the pool made the scrapes sting. Anna had also tripped and fallen in. She sat in the water next to Henry and hissed in pain, holding her ankle. It already looked swollen and bruised. The Reddimus box was still clutched in her free hand.

Henry sat up and pushed his wet bangs from his eyes.

"What is this?" he exclaimed.

"A salt pool. What's it look like?" Anna snapped. "I thought you would have figured that out by now."

"Please, I want to help you," Henry insisted. "It's a long walk to the road, and it'll be difficult with your ankle like that."

Anna looked at Henry's hand when he offered it, but instead she held the Reddimus box closer to her. "I'm not going to fall for your trick. You just want the box!" she said.

"Henry, are you okay?" called a voice. It was Jessie. She, Grandfather, Violet, and Benny had come to see if everything was all right. Because they hadn't been sprinting at top speed, they didn't

have any problems seeing the salt pool. Jessie and Benny waded into the pool and helped Henry up. They walked away from the pool a little so Henry could shake out the soreness from tripping. He even had grains of salt in his hair.

"We were worried!" said Benny.

"Thanks. I'm fine, but Anna's ankle is twisted," Henry said.

Henry heard footsteps. Other visitors were coming to see what was going on. He brushed himself off. Already, the saltwater was evaporating off him, and the little scratches on his knees and elbows didn't sting as much. It felt like they were evaporating too. Grandfather and Violet helped Henry sort out his clothes, which were disheveled from his fall.

"¿Qué pasó?" asked one of the shopkeepers as he arrived on the scene. "Is everyone all right?"

Another merchant said, "That was some race! Most excitement I've seen in years!"

"I'm fine," Henry said. "But there's someone who's been injured..."

The Aldens looked back to where Anna had been

sitting in the salt pool. She wasn't there anymore. When they looked up, they saw her limping away across the salt flat on her hurt ankle.

"Anna!" Jessie called. "You don't have to go out there by yourself!"

Anna didn't respond or turn around.

"Look," Violet said. She walked out into the salt pool. The water came up to just below her knee. She picked up the little box that was floating in the water. "The Reddimus box!"

"Do you think she forgot it, after all that?" Jessie asked.

Henry looked out across the salt flat, watching Anna walk glumly away. She looked to be taking the long way back to the road where all the cars were parked. But if she kept going at her current pace, they wouldn't have to confront her again. It seemed for the time being she had accepted defeat. That meant giving up the Reddimus box when she knew she couldn't get away with it.

"I don't know," Henry said. "I tried to help her, but she wouldn't let me...I just hope there's someone who she trusts."

A Clue and a Coordinate

They went back to the car. Benny looked out the rear window as they left Salinas Grandes behind. Henry opened his camera case. The last Reddimus box was nestled safely inside.

"Mr. Ganert can try to trick us all he wants, but the Argents aren't getting this box!" he said.

"I just hope we get another clue soon—a real one this time," said Violet as they drove down the mountain path back to Salta. She looked through the back window with Benny, but no red jeep came down after them. They had gotten the best of Anna this time, but the fact was she was in Argentina and working with Mr. Ganert. The Aldens would have to be clever and careful to

41

outsmart the two Argent agents.

Grandfather returned the car to the rental agency when they got to Salta. Then he asked the rental manager for directions to a nice hotel. By the time they got checked into their room, the sun had set behind the mountains. They had something to eat, and just as they were brushing their teeth and getting ready for bed, Henry got a text message. It was from Trudy!

Meet the contact tomorrow at noon, at the Casa Rosada next to the Plaza de Mayo, said the message. Henry read it out loud to his brother and sisters.

"What's the Casa Rosada?" Violet asked Jessie. "And Plaza de Mayo?"

Benny tilted his head. "Like...mayonnaise?"

Jessie laughed. "No, I don't think so. *Casa Rosada* means 'pink house' in Spanish, but it is also a famous building in Buenos Aires."

"Like the White House!" Benny said. "Does the president of Argentina live there?"

"Actually, yes, he does!" Jessie replied. "I remember from Spanish class when we watched a movie that took place in Buenos Aires. But I'm not sure what the Plaza de Mayo is."

"Hmm...the White House is near parks and plazas in Washington, DC," Violet thought out loud. "Maybe the Plaza de Mayo is a plaza near the Casa Rosada."

"I think you are right!" said Grandfather. "On my way to Buenos Aires to meet you, the person next to me was telling me about the fantastic historical sites near the Plaza de Mayo and the Casa Rosada. I'll book us an early flight back to Buenos Aires for the morning."

* * *

The next morning, once the Aldens' plane had lifted off, it was only two hours before it landed again in Buenos Aires. Although they had gotten up early to catch a flight, being in a new city was so exciting the children didn't feel sleepy at all. Grandfather waved down a taxi, and they were off toward the Casa Rosada.

Buenos Aires was a busy city humming with life. The roads were crowded with cars, buses, and pedestrians. Everywhere there were brightly painted buildings and street cafes with colorful patio umbrellas. Some of the cobbled roads were for foot traffic only.

"Look there! Tango dancers!" said Jessie, pointing. Two dancers performed in the street. The man wore a sharp black suit, and the woman was dressed in a flowing purple dress. Tourists watched as they danced to music played by a musician nearby. Grandfather asked the taxi driver to pull over so the children could watch for a minute.

"What kind of instrument is that?" asked Benny. "It's like a baby accordion!"

"It is called a bandonion," explained their taxi driver. "An essential tango instrument."

The two dancers moved gracefully to the music. The woman was wearing high heels, but she didn't trip once, even on the uneven cobbled road. When the song ended, the tourists applauded and whistled. Some threw coins in the hat near the bandonion player's feet. The taxi driver shouted "*¡Bravo, bravo!*" before driving onward toward the Plaza de Mayo.

"I want to learn to tango!" said Violet.

The taxi dropped them off at the Plaza de Mayo,

a square-shaped walking area the size of several city blocks. Many groups of tourists wandered the area, throwing coins into the fountains and taking pictures of the tall stone monument nearby. At the far end of the plaza was a huge mansion with many columns decorating the front. The mansion was colored salmon pink.

"The Casa Rosada!" said Benny.

"Wow, it really is pink, isn't it?" asked Henry.

The Aldens took their time exploring the plaza. There were gardens and palm trees and lots of pigeons. As the children and Grandfather neared the Casa Rosada, they saw a statue of a man holding a flag and riding a horse.

"That's Manuel Belgrano," Grandfather said. "He created the flag of Argentina."

"That must be why he's holding one!" Violet guessed.

"Is it just me, or does that man near the statue look like someone who might be waiting for us?" asked Jessie. Standing under the statue of Manuel Belgrano was a thin man in a purple suit. Even his felt hat was purple. When he saw four children

with their grandfather, he stood up straight and waved them over.

"You must be the Aldens," he said when they walked up.

"Yes...and you must be a friend of owls," Jessie said, looking at the man carefully. The owl was the symbol for the Reddimus Society. Asking someone if they were "a friend of owls" was the way Reddimus Society agents made sure they were talking to the right person.

The man smiled. "My name is Nicolás, and I am indeed a friend of the owls. But I fear you may have met someone who was not."

"I'm afraid so," Jessie said with a sigh. "A man gave us a fake clue at the airport. It sent us to Anna Argent, who tried to steal our artifact."

"Were you at the airport?" asked Henry.

"I was there," Nicolás said. "But I was at the wrong gate. It wasn't until I heard your grandfather's announcement over the loudspeaker that I figured out where you were. By the time I got there, you were all gone."

"Mr. Ganert must have gotten the gate changed

and sent that man with the clue!" Benny said.

"He probably planned on bringing us to Salta himself," said Henry. "But then Emilio distracted him."

Jessie nodded. "We should have been more careful, but we were in a hurry. The final artifact needs to be delivered as soon as possible."

"Well, I'm very glad you're all okay," said Nicolás. "I'm going to tell you the next clue. I heard that our operation might have been compromised by the Argents, so I haven't written it down. You'd do best to memorize it as well. If we don't have a written copy, it will be impossible for the Argents to steal the clue and use it for their own good."

The Aldens nodded. It made sense. If they received a clue on a piece of paper, Mr. Ganert or Anna might be able to steal it.

"Got it," Henry said. "We're ready."

The man cleared his throat and recited the clue:

You've been to one of me already,
The biggest ever built.
But I am much smaller,

A Clue and a Coordinate

So thin some call me an obelisk.
I am important for this place—
Look around and you will see.
When was I built?

After he finished, the man cleared his throat again.

"That is the clue. Do you have it memorized?"

"Can you repeat it one more time? I want to make sure we have it." Jessie looked at her siblings. "Let's each take a sentence. I will take the first one. Henry, you memorize the second sentence. Violet can take the third, and Benny can take the last one."

After the man repeated the clue, he asked them again if they had it memorized. They all nodded.

"Then I will say farewell. Best of luck in your mission!" Without another word, the man in the purple suit walked swiftly away. Grandfather chuckled after he had gone.

"The Reddimus Society sure knows how to dress snappy," he said. "I am going to get myself a nice purple suit when we get back to Connecticut...

ahem. So you kids got all that? I'm afraid I can remember only the first part."

"'You've been to one of me already,'" repeated Jessie. "'The biggest ever built.' We must be looking for an object like something we've already seen."

"Something that's the biggest of its kind," agreed Violet.

"'But I am much smaller, so thin some call me an obelisk,'" said Henry, repeating his sentence. "What's an obelisk?"

"I think it's a kind of monument," Jessie said. "The Washington Monument in Washington, DC, is an obelisk. It's very tall and has four sides, and it gets narrower as it goes up. On top it has a little pyramid."

"A pyramid!" said Benny. "We saw huge pyramids in Egypt. Aren't those the biggest pyramids ever built?"

Henry nodded. "That's right, they are! So we must be looking for a smaller pyramid...one so small it is more like an obelisk!"

"'I am important for this place,'" Violet recited. "That must mean Buenos Aires. 'Look around and you will see...'"

Henry, Jessie, Violet, Benny, and Grandfather looked around. They were glad for their sunglasses in the sunny afternoon plaza. Violet was the first to notice the statue at the other end of the plaza. They had already seen it when they'd arrived, but it wasn't until now that they thought anything of it.

"There, by where we came in!" Violet said. "The monument with the statue at the top!"

They hurried back down the plaza to take a closer look. The monument was solid and white, and Henry guessed it was more than fifty feet tall. It was the shape of a pyramid but much narrower than the pyramids in Egypt. It stood on a tall rectangular base. At the top was a statue of a woman holding a staff and a shield. She reminded Henry of the Statue of Liberty in New York.

"It does look a bit like an obelisk," Henry said. "But now that we're closer, I can see it's definitely a pyramid."

"The sign says this is called the Pirámide de Mayo," said Jessie. "The May Pyramid. This has got to be what the clue was describing."

"'When was I built?'" Benny chimed in with his sentence.

Jessie kept reading the sign. "It says it was erected in 1811. Should we try the code in the box?"

They were all excited to open the box, but Henry paused. There were many people all around. If they opened the box, Anna or any of Mr. Ganert's hired men would be able to steal it. As long as it was locked inside the box and the passcode was safe in their heads, it wasn't likely that they would lose the artifact.

"Let's find a restaurant for lunch," he said. "That way we can have some privacy while we figure this out."

Grandfather nodded. "I saw a nice-looking café up the street. I would love to try some Argentinian coffee."

"Let's go!" said Benny. "I want to know what's inside that box!"

The café was within walking distance, so they took in more sights on their way. Downtown Buenos Aires was full of people, cars, and beautiful architecture. Every building had columns or finely carved eaves or a fancy balcony. Jessie practiced her Spanish by reading the signs in store windows and on tour buses.

The café was right where Grandfather said it would be. Most of the customers were sitting outside on the patio, but Henry asked the hostess if they could have a booth inside where it was quiet. They ordered sandwiches and iced tea, and while they waited for their food, Benny wiggled his fingers energetically.

"The code!" he said. "Let's use the code to open the box! I want to see what's inside!"

"All right, all right." Henry laughed. From the booth, he could see the whole café. He was sure there were no Argent spies sneaking around. Henry slid his camera case over to Benny. "Go for it."

Benny and Violet opened the camera case together and took out the locked Reddimus box. It was finally time to open it and find out what the last artifact was. Everyone watched as Benny found the keypad and entered the four-digit code.

"One, eight, one, one," he said as he pressed the numbers. The box unlocked with a satisfying click. Benny carefully opened the lid and looked inside.

"What is it? What is it?" Violet asked eagerly.

Benny frowned and turned the box so they all could see.

"It's—it's—empty!" he cried.

"Shoot!" Henry exclaimed with dismay. "You don't think Anna Argent got into the box somehow, do you?"

Jessie reached inside and felt around. "Wait a minute. I think there's something in here," she said. After fishing around with her fingers, she pulled out a small strip of paper.

"Something's written on it," Violet said as Jessie put the paper on the table. "It's just numbers!"

"Hmm, not just numbers. Let me take a look," said Henry, turning the note toward him. "See here? There are dots in the numbers. And there is an S after one of the numbers and a W after the other one. I think these are coordinates."

"Coordinates?" asked Benny.

"Yes. They're numbers that represent a place on the world map. See, there are two numbers. One is latitude, which measures a distance north and south. The other is longitude, which measures distance east and west. With both numbers, we can find one place. Jessie, will you get your laptop out? We can find out where the coordinates point using the Internet."

Jessie did as Henry suggested. Benny wrung his hands, trying not to be too upset.

"Are you sure Anna didn't steal the artifact?" he asked.

"How could she have?" asked Henry. "She didn't have the code. These coordinates must just be the next part of the clue."

Jessie booted up her laptop. "That's different from all the other boxes, though. All the other boxes had the artifact right inside. I wonder why this time it's different."

"And Trudy said it was urgent we deliver the artifact as soon as possible," Violet reminded them. "Now the box is open, but we still don't have the artifact! I hope we don't run out of time."

Henry gave the paper with the coordinates to Jessie, who input them into an Internet map search.

"Don't worry," Henry said. "Let's find out where these coordinates lead and then go there right away. We've outsmarted the Argents all this time. There's no reason to worry now."

Jessie had finished looking up the coordinates on the map. She turned the laptop so everyone could see.

"Look here. It looks like the coordinates are pointing to a place just outside Buenos Aires. It's not very far at all."

Henry smiled just as the waiter appeared with their food. "See, Benny? No need to worry."

"Phew!" Benny said. "I was worried we wouldn't have a chance to eat!"

Jessie laughed. "Don't worry, Benny. We'll always find time for meals."

After they ate, Grandfather called another taxi. There were so many taxis in downtown Buenos Aires that all he had to do was whistle as one drove by. The Aldens got inside, and Jessie asked the driver if he could use coordinates in his GPS. After a minute, the man had entered the numbers.

"¡La reserva natural!" the driver exclaimed with a

smile as he started to drive.

"What did he say?" Benny asked.

"I think he said that we're going to a nature reserve," Jessie replied. "The words are kind of similar in English, aren't they? *Nature reserve, la reserva natural*?"

"Is that like an animal sanctuary, like the ones in Australia?" Violet asked. "I hope it is. I really liked seeing the kangaroos and koalas."

"What kind of animals come from Argentina?" Benny asked.

"Hmm," said Grandfather. "I suppose we might find armadillos. Or capybaras! Those are like giant guinea pigs."

Benny laughed at the idea of a giant guinea pig.

"I hope we find capybaras," he said.

"I hope we find armadillos!" Violet added. "What about you, Henry?"

"Me?" Henry asked. He laughed. "I hope we find the Reddimus artifact we're supposed to return!"

The Orange Orchid

The taxi driver dropped them off at the visitor center of the nature reserve. The reserve was very different from the busy city center of Buenos Aires. Instead of people and street music, there was only the sound of wind in the trees. Grandfather took a big breath and let it out with a content sigh.

"What a beautiful sight!" he said. "Isn't it surprising when a quiet place like this can be so close to a bustling place like the city? So, what's next?"

"Now that we're here, we've got to find out what we're looking for," said Henry. "We might be looking for another clue, but we could also be looking for a person. Keep your eyes peeled for owls and purple uniforms."

They went into the visitor center. Inside, there were rows with glass cases of delicate plants and flowers. The cases were lit with artificial sunlight. Some had mist sprayers that fogged up the window-panes. In front of the cases were little signs with information about each plant. Where the walls weren't covered with plants and flowers, they were decorated with woven textiles in many colors and geometric patterns.

"They're so beautiful," Violet said, peering at the flowers. Some were tall and wide, while others were small enough they might fit in the palm of her hand. Violet especially liked the flower called the Argentinian vervain, with dozens of tiny purple blossoms growing in fluffy clusters.

While Violet, Benny, and Grandfather looked at the flowers in the cases, Jessie and Henry puzzled over Henry's phone. He had found a phone app that allowed him to track their location on a map, just like the GPS in the taxi.

"Hmm," said Henry. "Even though we're very close to the coordinates we were given, we're not quite there yet. It looks like our real destination is out in the nature reserve."

"All right!" cheered Benny, who was listening nearby. "Let's go!"

They walked through the visitor center and out a set of doors on the other side of the building. Outside, they found themselves on a wide dirt trail that twisted off into a lush forest. The air was alive with birdsong, and in the distance they could hear the burbling of water. It was peaceful and quiet. It reminded Jessie a little of the woods where they had found their boxcar. Jessie doubted there was a boxcar sitting out in the Argentinian nature reserve, but the woods still made her feel at home.

"According to my phone, we should head this way," said Henry, and down the trail they went. They passed under low-hanging tree branches and stepped over moss-covered logs. The sunset twinkled through the leaves and shone in bright spots on the path. Benny ducked when something buzzed out of the trees and crossed the path right in front of them.

"Whoa!" he exclaimed. "Was that a giant bug?"

"No, look!" Violet said, pointing. The dark green

flying creature hovered just off the path. It was no bigger than a golf ball. "It's not a bug...it's a bird!"

"Oh, a hummingbird!" said Grandfather. "Would you look at that."

"I've never seen a bird so small...or a bug so big," Benny said. The hummingbird flitted back and forth, as if it were watching them. Its wings were moving so fast they were almost invisible. It chirped once then buzzed away into the trees.

"We're getting close," said Henry. He hadn't seen the hummingbird because his eyes were glued to the GPS on his phone. Jessie thought he looked very serious. She also knew how important it was that they find the Reddimus artifact quickly.

They followed the trail through the forest. Even though it seemed like they were hiking deep into the woods, the trail was well kept. Every once in a while, they saw a sign or a map, so they were never worried about getting lost. The trail wound around huge trees and alongside a little creek. Benny and Violet saw three more hummingbirds flitting through the trees.

After a while, the trail curved up a little hill

covered with fallen leaves and overgrown with white and purple wildflowers. It was quite a hike, and they were all a little winded by the time they neared the top.

"Oof, this is all the exercise I'll need this year!" joked Grandfather.

When they finally made it all the way up, they were surprised to find a small building with a glass roof. Three of the walls were made of glass too, and inside they could see the building was full of lush, green plants.

"This is definitely the place the coordinates point to," Henry said, catching his breath and putting away his phone. "Let's see if anyone's home."

They found a buzzer beside the door, and Henry rang it. Even though the walls were made of glass, the plants inside were so thick that it was difficult to see if anyone was inside. After a minute, Benny pointed when he saw something move inside. Someone was home after all! A blond man with a floppy hat and big glasses opened the door a crack and looked out at them. At first he didn't seem interested in meeting any strangers, but then his eyes went from Henry to Jessie to Violet to Benny.

"Four children..." he murmured to himself. "It could be them..."

Benny waved. "Hi, are you a friend of owls?" he asked cheerfully.

That was proof enough. The man opened the door all the way and let out a big sigh of relief.

"Yes, it must be you after all. Oh, thank goodness you're here," he said. "I've been waiting. Come in. Come in. My name is Hector—Hector Vargas."

The inside of the glass house was filled with plants. It didn't seem like the kind of house someone actually lived in. There were no beds or chairs in the single room. There was a sink, but it was full of plant pots and potting soil. A long metal table took up the middle of the room. It was covered in trays and pots of more plants. The glass ceiling let in the sunlight, so all the plants were green and happy. It smelled like leaves, flowers, and fresh dirt.

"Welcome to my greenhouse," said Hector. He glanced over his shoulder suddenly, as if he were nervous he'd made a mistake. "You are the Aldens, right?"

"Yes," said Henry. He introduced himself and his siblings. "And this is our grandfather. He's helping us while we're in Argentina, since we can't drive."

"And because I am wonderful company," added Grandfather with a wink.

"Wonderful to meet you all!" Hector called over his shoulder as he walked sideways through the tall, potted palms and hanging ferns. "Sorry there's nowhere to sit. Please wait here a moment. I've got something to give you."

As he moved farther away, Benny could see his clothes were spotted with potting soil, and there was even a leaf stuck to his shoulder. It almost looked like he was a plant disguised as a person.

"Finally!" Henry whispered. "I wonder if the artifact is a flower."

"Maybe that's why it wasn't in the box," Violet agreed. "Can you imagine? A poor flower stuck in that dark box this whole time! It probably would have withered up. No wonder there were only coordinates inside."

Hector came back with a clear glass box, and the Aldens could see they were right. Hector cleared a place on the center table and set the box down so they could all see the flower inside. It had long, green, oval leaves. A skinny green stalk grew up from the center of the leaves, and at the end of the stalk was an intricate, orange blossom.

"Oh my gosh," said Violet when she looked closely. "The flower looks like a monkey face!"

Indeed, the orange blossom had a cluster of petals in the center that looked like the face of a monkey or a baboon. There were even two dark spots where the eyes would be, and a darker petal in the center that looked like a nose.

Hector nodded. "Yes. It's called a monkey orchid. It's not a very creative name, I suppose, but it is definitely an accurate description."

"Wow! Is this the artifact we're supposed to return?" asked Benny. "Is it rare or valuable?"

Hector nodded.

"Something someone might try to steal and sell for a lot of money?" Henry added.

Hector nodded again.

"Monkey orchids are somewhat common, but this is the only specimen I've ever seen that's this color. They're usually white and peach, or sometimes dark red...So this orange orchid is incredibly rare. It would fetch quite a sum if it were put to auction. Plant collectors can be quite willing to spend a lot of money, and the rarer, the better."

"Where should we take it?" asked Henry. "We'll return it right away!"

This time Hector shook his head. "I wish I could tell you! It's not my orchid. I have known the Silvertons for a long time, so when I found this orchid on my greenhouse doorstep, I understood that I should take care of it until the Reddimus Society found out where it belonged. Oh, I should mention, the messenger left something else...I reckon it's a clue to help you figure out where you should take it."

Hector picked up a knotty rope from the table next to him. He handed it to Henry, who held it out for the others to see. It was a thin piece of white cord with dozens of other strands tied to it. Some of the strands were wrapped with green, silver, or gold knots.

"What is it?" Benny asked. "It looks like a piece of a sweater that came unraveled."

"There was only a simple note that came with it," Hector said. "All it said was, 'This khipu is the final key.'"

"Khipu? Huh?" Henry repeated. "I've never heard of that before."

Violet touched the soft pieces of rope. "I think it's pretty. It reminds me of the friendship bracelets I made in school with embroidery thread. But I still don't know what it means," she said.

"Didn't we see something like that in the building?" Benny wondered out loud.

"I think you're right," said Grandfather. "Next to all the flower cases there were some old-looking textiles with similar colors and patterns."

Hector rubbed his chin with his thumb in thought. "The visitor center wouldn't be a bad place to start looking. I don't think you'll find any clues out here!"

Benny looked at the monkey orchid in its glass case. It looked very breakable.

"We have to carry it in that?" he asked.

Hector nodded. "Yes, unfortunately. The monkey orchid is very delicate. It can't survive extreme temperatures. And since it's a tropical plant, it needs to stay inside this special container. If it's exposed to air that's too dry, it will become one sad little flower. I'm familiar with caring for orchids, as you can see from my greenhouse, but even I know that this plant needs to be with a specialist if it's going to be happy."

The Alden children looked at the orange orchid. It looked like it was looking back at them with its funny little monkey face. It was beautiful but fragile and very rare. No wonder Trudy had been told that returning the orchid was urgent.

"We'll do it," Henry said confidently. "Let's go to the visitor center, figure out what this khipu rope means, and get this little flower back where it belongs!"

A Knotty Puzzle

The Aldens walked with Hector back to the visitor center. Just as Benny had thought, the textiles that decorated the plant cases had many of the same colors and patterns as the rope clue. The children took turns looking at each of the draped fabrics and comparing them to the knotted khipu.

"We can assume the khipu is some sort of message," Jessie began. "Either that, or it's from the place where we're returning the orchid."

"Look at this one," Grandfather said, waving them over. He was looking at a tapestry that was done in red and gold. The tapestry was divided into six squares, and each square had a different number of birds woven into the design. The first square had only one bird, the second had two, and so on. Benny counted them.

"One square for each number of birds," he said. "All the way up to six!"

"I've seen this pattern before," Hector said. They all jumped at his voice. He had been off looking at plants since they got back to the visitor center, and they hadn't noticed him walk up. "It's a pattern that represents the migration of condors. Numbers and patterns were very important in ancient Incan art."

The children looked at the khipu. With all the knots and colors, it did seem like there was some kind of pattern to it.

"Ancient Incan, huh?" said Grandfather. "I wonder what language an ancient Incan message might be in. Would we even understand it?"

If anyone might have known the answer to that question, it would have been Hector—but the quirky botanist had already disappeared back among the rows of plants.

"All the tapestries here are based on ancient Incan art, but the khipu we have doesn't look like it's very old," Henry said, examining the knotted

rope. "The cord looks and feels like it's made of nylon or polyester. And the colors look like the embroidery thread Violet used to make friendship bracelets in school."

"Green, silver, and gold are the colors of Greenfield Elementary!" said Benny.

A Knotty Puzzle

"And junior high," Henry agreed. "They're the colors of our gym and our baseball jerseys."

"That can't be a coincidence," Jessie said. "So it was made recently, and in colors that had meaning for us. I don't think this is an ancient artifact. It's something made just for us!"

"Do you think the message is in English, then?" Violet asked, thinking about Grandfather's question.

The four of them took a closer look at the khipu. They stretched the main cord out in a line so the dangling strands fell down toward the floor. Benny counted the strands out loud until he reached twenty-two.

"It would make sense if each strand represented a letter," Jessie said. "It's a bit of a guess, but we have to start somewhere."

"Look. All of the strands have knots except for three," Violet said, running her fingers down the strands. "Maybe the strands without knots aren't letters, but spaces? I can't think of a single twenty-two-letter word, at least not in English."

"Good thinking, Violet. Let's make a chart to

keep track of this." Jessie took out her notebook and pencil. She marked twenty-two spaces, one for each vertical strand of rope. Next, she drew a line through the spaces that represented ropes with no knots.

"It looks like a hangman game," Benny said. "Except we don't have somebody to say when we get a letter right."

"Let's assume it's in English," Henry suggested. "There is probably a pattern. The only thing that sets the vertical strands apart is the knots. Maybe we should start with counting the knots."

It took them a while to count and record all the knots, but Benny enjoyed counting, especially when he could touch the knots as he went. In the end, they had written down a number under every space:

$$\underline{}\ \underline{}\ \diagup\ \underline{}\ \underline{}\ \underline{}\ \underline{}\ \underline{}\ \underline{}\ \diagup\ \underline{}\ \underline{}\ \underline{}\ \underline{}\ \underline{}\ \diagup\ \underline{}\ \underline{}\ \underline{}\ \underline{}\ \underline{}\ \underline{}$$
4 18 12 21 11 1 14 1 13 1 3 8 21 16 9 3 3 8 21

"All those knots almost made my eyes cross," Benny said, looking at the numbers and spaces.

"Good job counting," Jessie said.

A Knotty Puzzle

"Hey, I'm noticing a pattern," said Henry as he looked over the numbers. "None of these numbers goes higher than twenty-one."

"What does that mean?" asked Jessie.

"Well, there are twenty-six letters in the English alphabet. If this message is in English, maybe the knots represent letters of the alphabet. For example, A is the first letter, so if one represents A..."

Henry borrowed Jessie's pencil and made a few changes to the diagram:

$$\underset{4}{\_}\ \underset{18}{\_}\ \underset{}{\diagup}\ \underset{12}{\_}\ \underset{21}{\_}\ \underset{11}{\_}\ \underset{1}{A}\ \underset{14}{\_}\ \underset{1}{A}\ \underset{}{\diagup}\ \underset{13}{\_}\ \underset{1}{A}\ \underset{3}{\_}\ \underset{8}{\_}\ \underset{21}{\_}\ \underset{}{\diagup}\ \underset{16}{\_}\ \underset{9}{\_}\ \underset{3}{\_}\ \underset{3}{\_}\ \underset{8}{\_}\ \underset{21}{\_}$$

"There aren't any twos in the code, but there are a few threes," Violet pointed out. Henry nodded. Violet started to mouth the letters of the alphabet, counting on her fingers as she went. "The third letter of the alphabet is C."

The children went through each of the numbers and found out which letters went with which numbers. By the time they were done, they had a phrase: DR LUKANA MACHU PICCHU.

"After all that, I don't recognize most of these

words," Henry said. "I wonder if we did it wrong."

"*DR* means doctor," Benny said. "Maybe the rest is someone's name?"

"Well, it may just be Dr. Lukana," Grandfather said. "Machu Picchu is a famous place in Peru. I've seen photos of it. It's a stunning and sacred place. It's looking like that's the next place we're traveling to, eh?"

"If there's a Dr. Lukana in Machu Picchu, then yes," Henry said.

"Let's ask Hector if he knows of anyone by that name," Jessie suggested.

They called Hector back. He had opened one of the cases and was tending to some yellow orchids with a water dropper.

"Did you figure it out?" he asked when Benny called.

"Yes. We think it says Dr. Lukana, Machu Picchu," Henry said. "Do you know a Dr. Lukana?"

Hector straightened up and nodded, eyes widening.

"Yes! Of course, why didn't I think of that? Dr. Lukana is a Peruvian botanist, highly regarded in the breeding of rare specimens. She would be the perfect person to care for the orange monkey orchid. I didn't know she was in Machu Picchu now, but she has been known to do a fair amount of research in the Urubamba Province—quite near Machu Picchu, now that I think of it. It wouldn't be surprising if she were there. The area has some extremely interesting plant life!"

They hadn't known Hector for long, but this was the most excited they had seen him. He brought them to a map of South America near the welcome desk. It was a big map that included Peru, Brazil, Bolivia, and a little bit of Chile.

"This is Peru, between the western side of Brazil and the Pacific," Hector explained, pointing. "Machu Picchu is right here. Cusco is the nearest city with an airport. It is also the city where Dr. Lukana teaches. The last time I saw her speak, she was describing her research in the area around Machu Picchu. So really, if the clue is sending you that direction, it's likely you will be able to find her."

"Grandfather said that Machu Picchu is a sacred

place," Jessie said. "Is it a place that we're going to be able to visit?"

"There is a citadel there, and the location contains many ancient Incan ruins. But there are tour buses, and many people travel there," Hector said. "I think most people fly into Cusco and take a train to Aguas Calientes—which is also called Machu Picchu Pueblo. It's a small town near the ruins. If Dr. Lukana is nearby, someone there will help you find her."

"Thank you so much," said Jessie. "With this information, we're sure to find Dr. Lukana and return this orchid to her."

"You're welcome," Hector replied. "You might want to take a photo of the map. Just in case you need it. Cell phone service doesn't always work up in the Andes Mountains. Keep an eye on the weather too. It rains often, and the mud and everything can be tricky to get through."

Jessie took a photo of the map with her phone. If they lost reception, having a map stored would be helpful.

"We'll be careful," said Henry. "And Grandfather

will be with us. Right?"

Grandfather nodded. "You bet!"

Jessie packed up the khipu and her notebook into her backpack and pulled it over her shoulders. "Well, we'd better get going," she said. "The flight to Peru won't be a short one. If we can make it to the airport this evening, we can fly overnight and arrive by morning."

"We could return the monkey orchid as early as tomorrow!" Benny added.

Hector handed Henry the glass case container that held the monkey orchid. Henry used both hands to carry it, knowing that if he dropped and broke the case, the orchid wouldn't last long, especially once they left the nature reserve. It was exciting to have their last artifact in hand, but this was also the most fragile thing they'd had to return yet. They said thank you and good-bye to Hector, and he waved after them as they left the visitor center. Violet walked next to Henry so she could keep an eye on the little orchid in the glass case.

"I can't believe we're already returning the last Reddimus artifact," Violet said. "It seems like just yesterday we returned the little clay turtle to Christina Keene in New Mexico."

"You're right, it does." Henry sighed and looked at the orchid too. "But we can't get too excited. We still have a long way to go with this little guy, and we already know Mr. Ganert and Anna will be after it."

"Are we going to fly on the Reddimus jet?" Benny asked. "What if Mr. Ganert sees that we have the orchid? He might try to steal it."

"Do you think Emilio could manage the flight to Peru by himself?" Jessie asked. "What if we could somehow leave Mr. Ganert in Buenos Aires and fly straight to Cusco with Emilio? It's our final destination. As long as we return the orchid to Dr. Lukana in Machu Picchu, we won't need Mr. Ganert's help piloting the jet any longer. We could wait for Trudy to find another pilot to help Emilio fly us home."

Henry nodded. His eyes sparkled.

"I think I have a plan," he said.

CHAPTER

7

Into the Andes

When the Aldens got back to Buenos Aires, they thanked the taxi driver and returned to the city center. Henry wanted to do some quick shopping before they went back to the airport. They found a department store, and Henry gave Violet and Benny each some money he had saved from his own allowance.

"I want you both to pick out gifts for Emilio and Mr. Ganert to thank them for flying us all over the world," he told them.

"Why would we want to buy anything for Mr. Ganert?" Benny asked. "All he's tried to do is steal the artifacts from us!"

"That's not true," Henry explained. "He really

did fly us to each of our destinations, even if he is a spy. That helped us return the artifacts, either way."

Violet nodded. Then she waggled her eyebrows.

"Is this part of your plan, Henry?" she asked.

Henry winked. "Yes. But I still want you to pick out nice gifts for both of them. If it hadn't been for them, we wouldn't have been able to do such good work for the Reddimus Society."

Henry held on to the orchid case while he, Jessie, and Grandfather followed Violet and Benny through the department store. The shelves were stocked with all sorts of fun gifts, from toys to travel books, postcards, snow globes, and keychains. In the end, Benny picked out a joke book for Emilio. Violet picked out a box of chocolates for Mr. Ganert.

"Maybe something sweet will make him smile," she explained.

"Now, Jessie, why don't you pick out some nice gift bags to wrap them in," Henry said. "And be sure to get one extra gift bag that's the same size."

Jessie found some decorative bags and tinsel in the gift department. She even found two thank-you cards.

"What's the third gift bag for?" she asked, but Henry only grinned.

"You'll see!" he said.

Grandfather called a taxi, and they headed to the airport. When they arrived, Henry was the last person out of the cab. Jessie, Violet, Benny, and Grandfather waited patiently for him. Eventually he got out of the cab. In his hands were the three gift bags with the presents, topped with tinsel so no one could see inside.

"Where's the orchid?" asked Violet, noticing that he wasn't carrying the glass case.

"Don't worry," Henry assured her. "I have it."

They went through airport security and found the tram that would take them out to the tarmac where the private jets were parked. After a few minutes, the Reddimus jet came into view. Emilio and Mr. Ganert must have seen the tram coming, because they opened the hatch and headed down the stairs to meet the children as they exited the vehicle.

"Finally," Mr. Ganert said. "Did you find the artifact?"

"Here, Mr. Ganert, Emilio," Henry said. He

presented each of the pilots with a gift bag. "These are thank-you gifts from the four of us for all the help you've given in returning the Reddimus artifacts."

Emilio looked touched, his nose turning a little pink. "Why, thank you!" he said.

Mr. Ganert was not impressed. He didn't even look inside the bag.

"Yes, the artifact," he said. "Did you find it?"

"Oh no!" Henry said suddenly. He looked around. The third gift bag was nowhere to be seen. "I must have left it on the tram."

"Left it on the tram?" snapped Mr. Ganert, putting down his gift bag. He didn't seem interested in it one bit. He hadn't even said thank you. "You forgot a valuable artifact on the tram? No matter. I'll get it!"

Mr. Ganert sprinted after the tram as it drove away. It already had a big head start, and Henry didn't think Mr. Ganert would catch up to it until it stopped back at the airport gate.

"Come on, everyone," Henry said, picking up the gift bag that Mr. Ganert had left behind. "We've got to get going before Mr. Ganert gets back!"

"What?" Benny cried. "But the orchid!"

Henry opened the gift bag Mr. Ganert had abandoned and showed Benny the inside. Safely padded in the gift tinsel was the glass case holding the monkey orchid. The four children, Grandfather, and a confused Emilio clambered up the stairs into the jet.

"We're leaving without Mr. Ganert?" Emilio asked.

"Yes! We're headed to Cusco, Peru," Jessie explained, helping Henry close the hatch. Emilio nodded and saluted.

"Aye-aye, captains! I can make that flight by myself," he said before ducking away into the cockpit.

"What a trick!" Violet said as they buckled into their seats. "Henry, how did you know it would work?"

"Mr. Ganert is only interested in the artifact," Henry said. He took the orchid case out of the gift bag to make sure it was safe. "I knew he wouldn't care too much about a gift from us. But when he finds out the gift bag on the tram has his chocolates inside, maybe he'll decide to enjoy a sweet treat for himself while he's stuck here in Buenos Aires!"

Emilio was quick at the helm of the jet, and within minutes, they were zooming down the runway. There was a roar of jet engines and a little bump, and then they were in the air, headed to the last destination of their Reddimus mission.

The flight from Buenos Aires to Cusco was a journey filled with green, jungle-filled valleys and blue, misty mountains. The children watched the sunset as it filled the cabin with brilliant red and gold.

"This is Captain Emilio speaking," came Emilio's voice over the speaker. "Our current time of arrival is seven hours and forty-five minutes. I suggest you all rest up. We'll be landing in the morning, before you know it!"

Jessie found cozy blankets in one of the cabin storage compartments, and the four children and Grandfather curled up to sleep as the South American landscape passed by below.

The next morning, the Aldens awoke to their ears popping and the sound of the jet's engines changing to descent mode. The plane gently dipped below the clouds, and the children could see the airport below. Emilio made a smooth landing, and soon enough they were saying their good-byes on the jet's stairway.

"Good luck!" called Emilio as he waved to them. "Go get 'em!"

After they checked in with customs and had their passports stamped, Henry took out the map that Hector had given them.

"Hector said we can take a train from Cusco to a town called Aguas Calientes. From there, we take a shuttle up to Machu Picchu."

"I already booked our tickets on the train," said Grandfather, revealing five tickets that he'd hidden in his pocket. "I did it this morning while you were all still asleep! Come on, this way. We'll take a taxi to the station."

"I never realized traveling the world involved so many kinds of transportation," Violet said as Grandfather signaled a taxi at the front of the airport. They all got in, and Grandfather told the driver where they were headed. "Taxies, ferries, rental cars, airplanes..."

"And camels!" said Benny with a laugh.

"Don't forget the train that started our journey in Connecticut," Henry said. "I can't wait to see the train we're going to take up into the mountains. I'll bet it'll be something special."

The train was something special. When they reached the station, they could see it on the tracks. It was painted in a bright, royal blue with gold lettering and trim. Benny could hardly wait for Grandfather to check their tickets at the gate. When the five of them boarded, Benny and Violet gasped with delight.

The inside of the train was as fancy as the luxury restaurants they had seen on their journey, with velvety red seats and polished drink tables. Some of the cars had velvet-lined walls, while others were wood paneled with flowing white curtains. The passenger car in which their seats were assigned was wide and roomy, with big windows for looking through and tables between the chairs for playing games or reading books. In another car, they could hear a musician with a panpipe playing a cheerful tune.

"This is the best train I think I've ever seen!" exclaimed Benny as they took their seats. "Aside from our boxcar, of course."

Henry grinned. "Ha ha! Can you imagine our boxcar with velvet-lined chairs and all that fancy silverware from the dining car?"

"Yeah, it wouldn't be the same," Benny agreed. "I would still use my cracked pink cup!"

The children laughed at the thought, and then the train let out a loud whistle and eased forward. Benny and Violet, who got seats closest to the window, watched eagerly as the train left the station. Henry and Jessie watched too, while Grandfather sat across the aisle and looked out his own window.

Cusco was not very big, and within minutes, they were outside the city. First the train took them through flat farmlands, where the valley within the surrounding mountains was cleared in rich brown patches lined with stick fences. The mountains grew around them as the train passed over rivers and through dense forests, and soon they were going up into the Andes Mountains. Although the train tracks ran very close to the steep cliffsides of the mountains, the train felt sturdy and secure.

"It's almost like flying!" Benny said, looking out the window down the side of the mountain.

"Look at all the mist coming down from the mountains," Jessie said, pointing at the soft, rolling clouds of blue mist that faded in and out between the trees. "I wonder if it will rain?"

"Looks like it," said Grandfather. "It rains a lot in this area because of how the mountains are positioned near the ocean."

The mist soon turned to rain, as Grandfather predicted. The drops splattered against the big train windows, though it stayed comfortable and dry inside. The sky got darker, then lighter, then darker again, and when the heavier clouds came in, the rain fell harder.

Just when the storm seemed like it might ruin their mood, the musician with the panpipes from the other passenger car came into their car and began to play. He had been joined by another musician, this one a singer who played

an instrument that looked like a miniature guitar. They played and sang a peaceful, upbeat song in Spanish that made Violet want to dance, even though she didn't understand the words. The passengers clapped along with the musicians and forgot all about the thunderstorm outside.

When the musicians were finished, the passengers applauded, and the singer and piper took a bow. Benny clapped and remembered what he had heard in Buenos Aires when the tango dancers had finished their dance. He called, "¡Bravo, bravo!" and got a big smile and an extra bow from the musicians before they headed to the next car to continue their performance.

"Is the train slowing down?" Henry asked, looking out the window. They had been distracted by the music, but they could see that the mountains and trees were not moving by as quickly as they had before. After a few minutes, the train finally stopped altogether.

"Are we there?" asked Benny. "That was fast!"

"I don't think so," said Henry. "I don't see any village. I think we're stopped on the tracks in the middle of the mountains."

"Excuse me passengers. This is the conductor speaking...I'm afraid the rain has caused a mudslide on the tracks ahead. Once it's cleared we'll be able to resume our journey. Please enjoy our onboard entertainment and dining cars in the meantime, and see our attendants if you have any concerns."

"A mudslide!" Jessie said. "Wow, that sounds serious."

"Don't worry. It's actually quite common," said one of the train attendants who was checking in with the passengers.

"How long might it take to clear?" asked Henry.

"Hmm...sometimes it's not too long, only a couple of hours."

Henry took out the map that Hector had given them and spread it on the table. "Could you show us on this map where we are?" he asked.

The attendant pointed to a spot that was very near Aguas Calientes, only one or two miles away. "We were actually quite close to arriving, so it's a shame the storm couldn't have waited another ten minutes," she said. "But the good news is, once the track is cleared, we'll arrive in no time! Here, please enjoy a complimentary dessert."

The attendant gave them each a ticket for a free treat in the dining car and went to the next group of passengers.

CHAPTER 8

At Aguas Calientes

Henry sighed and looked at the dessert tickets.

"A couple of hours! Normally I would be happy for a free dessert, but we need to get this orchid to Dr. Lukana. Ice cream and cake aren't going to help us."

"It looks like it's only a couple miles," Jessie said, looking at the map. "We've easily walked that far between landmarks in other places we've been."

"If it's that close, we could hike," said Violet. "It's getting warm in here without the fans blowing. I'm worried about the orchid. What if it gets too hot?"

"We haven't watered it either," Benny added. "I bet it's thirsty."

Henry tapped his chin, deep in thought. It was

definitely getting stuffy in the train, and when he opened his backpack to check on the orchid, he thought it was looking a little wilted. The case was sealed shut, so it hadn't gotten any water since they had left Hector's the previous day. Each of the little monkey faces drooped. The orchid needed an expert to take care of it, and soon.

"It's a couple miles if we were to take the train, but if we were to hike it, it would actually be much shorter. The train has to take a certain path that goes through the mountains. If we hiked, we could go straight up, and it would be less than a mile."

"What do you think, Grandfather?" Jessie asked.

Grandfather leaned across the aisle to look at the map and then leaned the other way to look out the window, up the mountain forest. The rain was already clearing up, and the sun was peeking out from behind the clouds.

"Hmm...in my youth I would have done it lickety-split. But I think I probably wouldn't have the best time. The four of you could certainly make it if you were careful and stayed together," Grandfather said.

At Aguas Calientes

"Then we'll do it," Henry said, packing up the map. "Grandfather, we're going to hike up to Aguas Calientes. We'll take the shuttle to Machu Picchu and find Dr. Lukana. We'll meet you back in Aguas Calientes after we return the orchid."

"Then we will all go back to Machu Picchu the next day, so I can see it!" said Grandfather. "I didn't come all the way out here to miss out on such an opportunity, you know!"

Henry, Jessie, Violet, and Benny all stood up and got their things together.

"All right, then we'll go!" Henry declared.

"I'll come with you to make sure the attendants don't think you're out of your minds," Grandfather said, standing with them. "Most kids probably wouldn't choose hiking a mountain over a free dessert!"

"If we didn't have to return the orchid, I would probably take the free dessert," admitted Benny.

At first the attendant told Grandfather that the Aldens couldn't leave the train. But after Grandfather explained the situation and promised that they were all responsible and used to roughing it in the woods, she finally spoke to the conductor about it. The conductor took a look at the monkey orchid and nodded.

"All right, I understand," he said. "But please be careful!"

"Be safe," added Grandfather. "And take this. It's old-fashioned, but there's a reason sailors and other travelers kept them long before cell phones and GPS!"

Out of Grandfather's pocket came a little brass compass. He put it in Henry's hand. Henry turned it back and forth and watched the needle move so it was always pointing north.

"Thanks, Grandfather," Henry said. "See you in Aguas Calientes."

"Enjoy our free dessert!" added Benny.

Stepping out of the train into the mountain forest was cool and refreshing. The storm clouds had passed, and the sky was nearly sunny again, though raindrops still dripped from every leaf and branch. Henry held the compass in one hand and the map in the other, turning left and then right until he knew which way to go. Then he started up

the mountain, and the others followed.

Climbing the mountain was more difficult than other hikes the four children had taken. When they had lived in the woods in their boxcar, they had explored often and learned how to grab hold of roots and branches when the trail got steep. But here in the Andes, everything was still slick from the rain, and at times the forest was almost vertical. Henry and Jessie helped Benny and Violet up over rocks and the remains of stone walls.

Luckily, there wasn't any more rain, so by the time they came across a road, they were only winded but not soaked. They could hear car engines and people talking. So they followed the noises and soon found themselves in a small village that could only be Aguas Calientes. There was a center square surrounded by orange, red, and white buildings. Many of the restaurants had outdoor tables and chairs, though no one was sitting outside because the chairs were still wet from the rain.

"We made it!" Henry said. He was the most energetic and least out of breath, though he still flopped down to rest on the first bench he saw. "Whew! What a hike."

"I'm just glad we made it," Violet said, sitting beside him.

Henry checked on the orchid in his backpack. It was still looking droopy, but the glass case was intact. If they could find Dr. Lukana soon, it would be fine.

"Why don't you three wait here and rest, and I'll go find out when the next shuttle to Machu Picchu leaves," he said. "Don't get too comfy. We've got to leave on the next shuttle so we can find Dr. Lukana."

Henry walked down the main road toward a little station by the train tracks. There were signs advertising the shuttle buses that went to Machu Picchu, and when he got closer, he saw a station attendant reading a newspaper in the booth.

"Excuse me, when is the next shuttle?" Henry asked.

"Not until the roads are cleared. The rain downed a few trees, and it wouldn't be safe to drive the shuttles."

The Khipu and the Final Key

Henry sighed in disappointment and ran his hand through his hair.

"You don't happen to know of a Dr. Lukana who is working near Machu Picchu, do you? She is a botanist. I'm looking to return something to her."

"Oh yes, Dr. Lukana! She takes the shuttle down from her lodge when she comes to town. A very nice woman."

The good news was a relief after hearing the shuttle wasn't running, and Henry's hope was renewed. "That's great! A lodge, you said? You mean at Machu Picchu?"

"Yes. There's a very nice lodge up there where she stays when she's researching." The attendant must have noticed Henry was in a hurry. He looked at Henry's muddy hiking shoes and backpack and said, "Looks like you don't have a problem going by foot, eh? It's supposed to be good weather for the rest of the day, and it isn't far if you're up for it—about a kilometer and a half. Takes about an hour. The trail starts over there, and there are plenty of signs...Once you get there, you can't miss the lodge."

At Aguas Calientes

"Thank you so much!" said Henry, and he returned to his siblings with the good news.

"More hiking?" Jessie said, after Henry had explained. "Bring it on! A kilometer and a half... What is that, about a mile? That's not too bad at all, especially if the weather is supposed to stay nice. Let's go!"

The hiking trail to the Machu Picchu site was well marked with wooden signs. There were a couple other travelers making the trek by foot. At first, the path was fairly even, running along a river and across a bridge. Soon after, though, the four Aldens were climbing up a long row of steep stairs built into a wall of gray, stone bricks. The stairs were so steep, at some points they were climbing with their hands as if they were going up a ladder.

"I see why it takes an hour, even if it's only a mile," Violet said, wiping some sweat from her forehead. "We're climbing straight up the mountain!"

The sun was warming the rain-soaked forest, and it was getting sticky. But there was still some mist hiding in the shade of the trees that was cool and refreshing.

The Khipu and the Final Key

Every once in a while, the rocky stairs leveled off along a road. Henry said it was probably the road the shuttle took when it was running. There were a few fallen trees and some rocks and mud littering the road, so it was clear why it was unsafe to drive on. From the road, they could look out over the side of the mountain. Aguas Calientes was hidden by the thick trees, even though they knew it was down there, somewhere.

"According to that sign, we're halfway there!" Henry said, pointing.

"I'm going to sleep good tonight!" Benny said, huffing with effort.

They hiked for another half hour. Nearly right on the dot, their path widened and they could hear people's voices coming from up ahead. They followed the sounds and soon arrived at a landing. A handful of tourists were looking out over the mountain cliff and taking pictures. The Aldens walked up to join them and took in the view.

"Wow," whispered Jessie.

Spread out on a gentle slope were the remains of several dozen ancient buildings. None had roofs, but their stone foundations were well preserved. Even from the distance, the children could see window and door holes left in the building walls. Green grass grew flat and soft between the buildings, and a fresh-scented breeze wafted through the tree-covered mountains that surrounded them.

"It's gorgeous!" Benny said. "Whoa, check out that thing!"

A tall, brown, fluffy animal was wandering through the building remains. It had a long neck and looked sort of like a camel, but without a hump.

"A llama!" Violet said. She put on the sunglasses Grandfather had bought her in Salinas Grandes. They helped her see better as the clouds continued to clear from the sky. She watched the llama walk peacefully through the old walls. It didn't seem to mind all the human visitors who were exploring the ruins.

"After we return the orchid, I definitely want to explore," Jessie said. "But let's put our priorities in order. Let's find that lodge where Dr. Lukana is staying."

"The station attendant said we can't miss it," Henry said. From where they stood on the landing, they scanned the mountainside near the site. All of the buildings that were part of the site were so old their bricks had turned white from the sun. But one building that was off to the side was modern and new.

"That's probably it," Benny said with a goofy smile. "It's the only building with a roof and glass in the windows."

They found a path that led to the lodge. It was a short walk from the main landing where they had arrived. Up close to the building, they could see that the sign read Machu Picchu Luxury Lodge. On the front lawn, overlooking the site, were deck chairs shaded by big bushes with white, hanging flowers.

"This is probably the fanciest hotel we've seen yet," Violet whispered to Benny as they walked up the front steps.

"The ones back in Aguas Calientes looked pretty fancy too," Benny said.

The young man at the reception desk smiled and

greeted them when they walked in. Henry cleared his throat and went up to the desk.

"Excuse me, we're looking for Dr. Lukana. She's a botanist who stays here," he said. "Can you page her for us?"

"Oh, are you the Alden family?" asked the receptionist. "Dr. Lukana told us you would be coming. She left a message for you...here you go." The receptionist handed Henry an envelope. Henry thanked him and went back to open the envelope with his siblings. Inside the envelope was a message and a plastic hotel key card.

Henry read the message aloud: "'Dear Aldens: Forgive the inconvenience, but I have been delayed and will not be able to meet you until tomorrow morning. Please enjoy my accommodations at the lodge until I arrive. Signed, Dr. Lukana.' This key card must be to her room."

"Let's go drop off our stuff and take a rest," suggested Jessie. "I'd like to get this backpack off, and my legs are sore from all the hiking."

The Other Silverton

They found the room that matched the number on the key card. It was well furnished with plush beds and pillows. Scattered all over the room were books and research notes. A big window on one side of the room looked out over Machu Picchu.

In front of the window were a few glass cases like the one that protected the monkey orchid. They all had other orchids inside, in a rainbow of colors. Henry took the monkey orchid out and gave it a look.

"How does it look?" Violet asked.

"Better than before, but I still hope Dr. Lukana is able to take care of it soon," Henry said as he set it beside the other orchids. "At least it's in good company now."

"Did we do it?" Benny asked. "Did we return the last artifact?"

The four Aldens looked at the monkey orchid sitting on the windowsill with the other orchids. It fit right in.

"I think we just might have," Henry said. "But let's wait to make sure everything is explained to Dr. Lukana before we sign off just yet."

"I saw a sign in the lobby that said the lodge has Wi-Fi," Jessie said as she took out her laptop. "I want to send a message to Grandfather to let him know that we're safe at a lodge up by Machu Picchu. I'll tell him we'll meet him in Aguas Calientes tomorrow. He would worry if he got to the town and waited for us and we never showed up."

Henry nodded. "Good idea. Maybe we should send an email to Trudy too."

They all jumped at a knock at the door. Henry went to the door and looked through the peephole. He chuckled when he recognized who was on the other side.

"Jessie, don't worry about that email," he said. He opened the door. Standing in the hall was

Grandfather, and with him was a woman with purple-dyed hair. She looked just like Trudy Silverton, except she didn't have a cast or a broken leg.

"Hello, Henry," she said with a smile. "Jessie, Violet. Hello, Benny! It's nice to finally meet you. I'm Trudy's sister..."

"Tricia Silverton!" the Aldens exclaimed at the same time.

Tricia laughed and came into the lodge room with Grandfather. She noticed the monkey orchid on the windowsill and nodded approvingly. She sat in the wicker chair near the window and folded her hands across a knee.

"I'm sure you all have a lot of questions for me. I figured that since you had managed to bring the monkey orchid here, it was time that I finally meet you and thank you for your hard work...and explain what's been going on."

"I think we figured some of it out," Jessie said. "You were giving us clues about how to return the artifacts so the Argents wouldn't be able to stop us. Right?"

Tricia nodded. "Exactly. You see, a long time

ago, the Reddimus Society used to return items matter-of-factly. But items started to go missing—stolen, before they could be returned. It's been that way ever since Trudy and I started working for the Reddimus Society. I decided it was time to put an end to it."

"And by keeping the information about the artifacts a secret, it was easier to figure out who the spy was," Violet said. "That's how we figured out it was Mr. Ganert."

"But why didn't you just tell us you thought there was a spy in person?" Henry asked. "It seemed like you had just spoken to Wenwen before we met her in China..."

"And I thought I saw you in Rome!" Violet remembered.

Tricia sighed. "I'm sorry it seemed so mysterious. The truth is, while the Argents were trying to keep you from returning artifacts, they had also started trying to take new ones. They took an artifact in Kenya, a ruby ring in France, and an artifact in Japan. I was trying to stop these thefts and help you return the artifacts at the same time. Unfortunately, because I was following the Argents around, Agent Carter and the others started to wonder if I might be working *with* them. I needed to stay hidden until we could prove who the real spy was."

"Mr. Ganert!" Benny said.

"What happened to Mr. Ganert, anyway?" Henry asked.

"Well, after I heard from Trudy that you had

discovered it was him, it was easy to prove by looking through his records. I even found out the letters in *Ganert* can also spell *Argent*...He's not a very creative fellow, is he?" Tricia laughed. "Now, how about I thank you for figuring out who the spy was, and for returning the final artifact, by treating you all to supper? The lodge has a wonderful chef. I think you'll all enjoy it!"

The lodge had an outdoor patio covered with a trellis. The dinner special was grilled citrus chicken with rice. The food was served with a fried vegetable that looked almost like a banana.

"These are fried plantains. A Peruvian tradition!" Tricia explained.

Benny took a big bite. The plantains tasted more like a sweet potato than a banana, but it was tasty either way. "Mmm! Delicious!"

It was fun, but a little weird, to have Tricia right there in front of them. It was like they had already known her a long time, even though they had just met her! In a way, she had been with them on their travels the whole time. Henry thought back on all the secret messages and clues they had received.

Each one had been from Tricia, leading them in the right direction.

"Thank you," Henry said, "for helping us do a good job returning the artifacts. We couldn't have done it without you."

Tricia shook her head. "I should be the one thanking you. The truth is, I'm the one who couldn't have done it without the four of you."

For dessert they had another Peruvian dish called *tres leches*. Jessie translated it from Spanish.

"Three milks?" she asked.

"Yes! It's made with three kinds of milk. Two kinds of condensed milk and heavy cream...oh, look at it!" Tricia said when she saw the waiter bring out the cake. "I'm hungry all over again!"

The cake was fluffy and white, with vanilla frosting and red cherries on top. It was very sweet and moist, almost like bread pudding. The six of them ate up every last bite. When they were full, Tricia and Grandfather sipped mugs of coffee while the children drank hot chocolate spiced with a dash of cayenne pepper.

"Ooh, look at those storm clouds rolling in,"

Tricia said, glancing to the sky beyond the mountains. "The rain from earlier might have just been a little teaser."

"Is it safe to be up here during a storm?" Violet asked.

"Safe? Absolutely. And better than safe. Storms when you're in the mountains are simply amazing!" Tricia said with a big smile. "I'll bet you've never seen a rainstorm like the one you'll see tonight, if those clouds are headed our way."

They watched the dark purple clouds roll across the sky toward them as the sun set. The temperature fell quickly until it was just cool enough to make goose bumps on Benny's arm. Soon, rain pattered down in big drops, and they went inside before they got drenched.

"You four are welcome to stay in Dr. Lukana's room tonight. I've rented two more rooms, one for myself and one for Mr. Alden. Please come and find me if you need anything. In the morning, we can explore Machu Picchu and return to Cusco together...I'm sure Emilio would like to be let in on what's been going on this whole time too."

The Khipu and the Final Key

"He's been a good sport, even when we thought he might be the spy," Henry said. "Good night, Tricia. It was great to finally meet you. We'll keep the monkey orchid company tonight until Dr. Lukana makes it back…"

The children went back to their room and got ready for bed. But just as Henry was about to turn out the lights, a loud crack of thunder shook the windows. The lights flickered and went out.

"Was that you, Henry?" Jessie asked. "Or did the power just go out?"

"It looks like it's the power," Henry said, flipping the light switch up and down. "Let's see if Tricia or Grandfather have electricity."

The children put on the four pairs of slippers that were near the door. Then they went out into the hallway. Tricia and Grandfather were already there.

"Looks like the lights are out everywhere," Grandfather said.

"When will they come back on?" asked Benny nervously.

"I'm sure it will be fixed soon, Benny," Tricia

said. "In the meantime, since the lights are out, let's go enjoy the show. This is the kind of storm you can only dream of experiencing."

Tricia took Benny's hand and led everyone through the lightning-lit hallways to a common area with big, thick windows. Outside, the rain fell in sheets and the sky was dark, but the lightning and booming of thunder were impressive. Holding on to Tricia's hand, Benny watched the sparkling lightning light up the mountains.

"It's kind of like fireworks," Violet said.

"Isn't it?" Jessie said. "Just like the Fourth of July!"

They watched the lightning flash in purples and blues and whites. After a few minutes, the roughest part of the storm was over.

"Hmm. Too bad—looks like the power is still out," said Grandfather. "Now that it's night, it's pretty dark. I wish I had brought a flashlight."

"Yes, sorry," said one of the lodge clerks. He was hurrying by in a rain poncho, holding a flashlight in one hand. "The storm knocked down a power line. We're working on getting the backup generator working. We'll be up and running as soon as we can!"

The clerk waved and went out into the rain, flipping on his flashlight. Its yellow beam cut through the darkness as he went around the back of the lodge. Benny got an idea and dug into his pocket. Out came the travel-size flashlight he had gotten from Trudy back when they had first found out about the Reddimus Society.

"Did you get that from my sister?" Tricia asked.

Benny switched it on. Even though it was small, it had a nice, bright light. Violet had hers too, and together they were able to light their way down the hall toward their room.

"Yeah. She said they would come in handy!" Benny said.

"Looks like she was right," Tricia said.

"Will you four be all right?" Grandfather asked. "They'll get the power on soon. In the meantime, it might not be a bad night to tell some ghost stories. Ha ha!"

"Between Violet and Benny's flashlights, I think we'll be fine," said Jessie. "Good night!"

"Good night!" said Tricia. "Sleep tight. See you in the morning."

Jessie and Henry followed Violet and Benny back to their hotel room. The thunder and lightning had all but passed. The only thing left of the storm was the soft tapping of rain on the roof. When they reached their room, Henry stopped to get the key card from his pocket.

"What a great storm," Benny said. "And we returned the orchid, and we got to meet Tricia. She's fun!"

"Wait a moment, Henry," Jessie whispered. "Look."

They all hushed and looked where Jessie was pointing. The door to their room was open slightly. Jessie was sure she had closed and locked it when they had left. When she leaned in to listen, she could hear someone rustling around. She exchanged glances with Henry, Benny, and Violet. They all nodded at each other in agreement. Then Henry and Jessie opened the door, and at the same time, Benny and Violet aimed their flashlights into the dark room.

The Khipu and the Final Key

A woman with a blond ponytail froze when the light beams landed on her. It was Anna Argent, and in her hands was the glass case containing the monkey orchid.

We Return

"Wait! Stop right there!" Henry yelled.

Anna didn't waste any time. As soon as they recognized her, she turned and made a break for the closest window. She was so fast that Benny and Violet lost her with their flashlights, and then—

"Ouch!"

There was a crash. Then the power came back, and the lights flickered on. In the middle of the room, Anna was bent over, holding the ankle she had twisted at Salinas Grandes. It appeared she had lost her footing and tripped over a solid wood chair in the dark.

The orchid case was on the floor. The orchid was safe, but a big piece of glass had broken out of

one side of the case.

"Oh no!" said Violet. She and Benny didn't need their flashlights anymore, so they put them away. Violet went to grab the orchid case, but Anna got hold of it first. She moved toward the window. Her limp had come back after stumbling again on her injured ankle.

"Stay right where you are," she said. Her eyebrows were crinkled in pain. "I'm taking this orchid to the Argents, and you can't stop me!"

"No, wait," Jessie said. "You're hurt, and it's dangerous out there!"

"You don't care about my safety. I don't believe it!" Anna said, though she looked like she was taken off guard. It reminded Henry of the way she had looked at him at the salt flats. It was as if she wanted to believe them but couldn't.

Benny shook his head. "No way! It's the truth. The rain probably caused all kinds of mudslides on the road. It's so dark, and there could be another storm!"

"You could get more hurt," Violet agreed.

"You're just trying to trick me. All I've tried to

do is steal from you! There's no reason you would keep trying to help me after all I've done."

Anna backed away from them. She put her hand on the chair as if she were planning to use it to break the window and escape.

"If you don't believe us, then at least think about it this way," Henry said, trying to convince her. He remembered how defensive she could be, and he didn't want her to do anything that might set her off. "You can't take the orchid out with a broken case. The air is too cold—the orchid will die. How much money do you think you can get for it then?"

Anna frowned and looked at the case. She saw the big hole broken in the glass and realized Henry was right. The look on Anna's face changed from determined to worried.

"Please don't go," Benny said.

"Then you only care about the orchid!" Anna snapped. "If—if I leave it here, will you let me go?"

The Aldens exchanged glances. Anna had been following them, trying to steal the artifacts since the beginning of their journey. It was almost as if she, like Tricia, had been a part of their group, in a way.

"Yes, we won't stop you," Henry said. "But you don't have to go. Like Benny said, it's dangerous out there. We're at the top of a mountain. You should stay here overnight or you could get lost or seriously hurt."

Anna looked back at them for a long time, clutching the broken orchid case. Then all at once she let out a big huff. She sat down in the chair and set the orchid down on a nearby table. She and the Aldens looked up when they heard footsteps. Tricia Silverton looked inside and gasped.

"What is going on? I heard a crash and some shouting...Anna, what are you doing here?"

"She was returning the monkey orchid. Right?" Henry said.

"Sure," said Anna glumly. "If you want to look at it that way."

"You were trying to steal it, weren't you?" Tricia asked. "That's just like you Argents!"

"We wouldn't have to steal if it weren't for you Silvertons!"

"Stop fighting!" Benny said, louder than both Anna and Tricia. They were quiet and listened to him, although they turned their noses up at one another. They also had matching, bright red cheeks. "Anna decided not to steal the orchid, so it doesn't matter!" Benny continued.

"It'll be returned to Dr. Lukana tomorrow, and Anna will go on her way," Jessie added.

The room was very quiet for a minute. Anna crossed her arms. Tricia did too. Then she chuckled with a little sigh.

"Sheesh. Look at us, fighting like old times. What would Grandfather think?"

"Grandfather?" Violet asked, confused. "Our grandfather?"

Tricia shook her head. "No. Our grandfather, Silas Argent. Anna and I are cousins."

"What?!" Benny gasped.

Anna unfolded her arms and clasped her hands in her lap.

"It's true. Trudy, Tricia, and I grew up together. We were rather close. But while the Silvertons had wealth, the Argents didn't. We did what we had to do to make ends meet. Sometimes that included selling valuable artifacts. Grandfather Argent didn't condone it. He tried to talk us out of it...but he didn't understand."

While Anna spoke, Tricia reached into her pocket for her wallet. Inside she had a photo of three young girls smiling with their grandfather. The girls were Trudy, Tricia, and Anna. Their grandfather had silvery gray hair that stuck out from below a purple cap. He had a big smile, and Benny could see one of his front teeth was capped in silver.

"That man!" Benny said. "He's the one who put the clay turtle in our house! The pirate!"

Tricia laughed. "Did he tell you he was a pirate too? Yes, this is our grandfather, Silas Argent. We hadn't heard from him for many years. You see, he is the one who started Argent Auctions. When he did that, our family split apart. That's when Trudy and I stopped seeing Anna. But when he was responsible for leaving that porcelain turtle in your house, it started everything into motion."

"Grandfather Argent changed his mind about

the auction," Anna said. "He started to think that selling off the artifacts was wrong and wanted to stop doing it. But without that income, our family wouldn't be able to take care of itself. I didn't know what he was thinking, bringing that turtle to you."

"I think he was hoping it would show you there was another way," Tricia said. "He was trying to lead by example and show that the right thing to do was return the artifact, not sell it. By doing something drastic, he hoped he would get everyone else to change their minds too, including you, Anna."

Just then Jessie remembered something that Trudy had told them about Tricia. She had said Tricia had been seen talking to Anna in Japan. At the time, it hadn't made any sense why the two might have been speaking. Now she wondered how it was all connected.

"Tricia, did you really talk to Anna in Japan?" she asked.

"Yes. I was trying to talk some sense into her," Tricia said. "I didn't want any more artifacts stolen. I wanted her to do the right thing."

Anna nodded. She looked like a balloon with

all the air let out. "But I didn't listen. And a lot of good it has done me. I wasn't able to stop you from returning one single artifact, even with Mr. Ganert's help."

"That reminds me," Violet said. "How did you find us here in Machu Picchu? We left Mr. Ganert back in Buenos Aires. He had no idea where we were headed."

"Oh, I've known where all the artifacts were going from the very beginning," Anna said. "Tricia and Trudy are very clever, but sometimes even they mess up. The map with all of the stolen item locations was glued to the inside of your old trunk. I saw it when I snuck onto the train that first night."

"The scribbles and coffee stains!" Benny exclaimed, remembering. They had seen a blotchy pattern on the inside of their grandfather's trunk, but it had been very dark and they had thought it was only spilled coffee.

"Consider it our gift to you," Tricia said. "You might not have been able to visit Machu Picchu otherwise!"

The Khipu and the Final Key

There was an awkward silence. Then, surprising them all, Anna Argent laughed.

"Yes. I guess you're right. I've traveled more in the last few weeks than I have in all my life. Even if I didn't get away with a single one of your artifacts, I guess I got to visit a lot of places I wouldn't have gone to otherwise."

"Like the pyramids," Benny said.

"And the Salinas Grandes," Violet added.

Anna rubbed her face with her hands. The blush in her cheeks was fading.

"Tricia, do you think Grandfather Argent will forgive me?" she asked.

"Of course he will! After all, you didn't stop us from returning any of the artifacts." Tricia winked and then added more seriously, "Listen. I spoke with Agent Carter when we had to straighten all this out. I explained your situation. He said that if you and the other Argents want to make things right, you first need to give yourselves up and return all the artifacts you've helped steal. Agent Carter knows you are good at tracking down artifacts. He said that if you use your skills to help the Reddimus

Society return stolen artifacts, eventually you can pay off your debt that way."

"It won't be easy to convince all of the Argents," Anna said, but still she looked hopeful. "But...I will try." Then she gave a little sniffle. "I hate to admit it, but the truth is, after following the Aldens all this time and watching them help each other, I started to miss spending time with you and Trudy. We used to be such good friends...I'd like to be good friends again."

Tricia turned toward her cousin. Her expression softened.

"I'd like that too," she said. "Come on. You look tired from sneaking all the way up here to find the orchid. I rented a big room and you can share it with me. It'll be like old times when we used to have sleepovers."

Anna laughed at the idea, but she looked happy and relieved. She stood when Tricia waved her toward the door. Before she left, she turned back to the Aldens.

"Sorry about all the trouble I've caused," she said.

"It's all right," Benny said, giving her a big smile.

The Khipu and the Final Key

"It made things a lot more exciting!"

After Tricia and Anna left, Jessie closed and locked the door. It was getting late. The sky was pitch black outside the window, since there were no city lights up in the mountains. Violet inspected the broken glass case that held the monkey orchid.

"I think the orchid will be all right until tomorrow," she said. "It's cool outside, but it's not bad in here. All the other orchids look pretty happy, anyway."

"Then let's get some sleep," suggested Henry. "It's been a long day."

They all slept well after the hiking and climbing they had done. Jessie dreamed about humming-birds and orchids, and she woke to the sound of little bells. At first she thought maybe she had dreamed their entire adventure and that she was back home, where Violet had hung a mobile in her room.

When she opened her eyes, she saw the room full of orchids. Out the window, the lush mountains and Machu Picchu greeted her. The sound of bells was the jangling of keys outside the hotel door.

"Good morning!" came Grandfather Alden's voice. "Are you kids up?"

We Return

Jessie opened the door and waved him in. Violet, Benny, and Henry were just waking up. "Yes, we're up...sort of. Good morning!"

"I heard from Tricia what happened last night. She and Anna Argent went out to find Dr. Lukana already. Tricia told me to get you four and the orchid and meet them."

The children got ready to go, and Benny took a turn carrying the orchid. Even though the glass case was broken, the air was warm when they walked outside and down the path to Machu Picchu. The orchid looked happy to feel a little fresh air, its leaves and orange blossom perking up like it was smiling.

The Aldens found Tricia and Anna talking to an older woman, down by Machu Picchu in a grove of trees. It was strange to see Anna standing out in broad daylight, not trying to hide or sneak around. In fact, she looked a lot like Tricia and Trudy.

"Good morning, Aldens!" said Tricia cheerfully. "This is Dr. Lukana."

"Hello," Dr. Lukana said. She looked at the orchid. "Oh, there it is! Oh my, what a lovely specimen. May I see it?" Benny handed the orchid to Dr. Lukana. The botanist turned the case back and forth, eyes wide in awe as she examined it. "It's in great condition. You four did a fantastic job keeping it safe all the way from Argentina. Yes! Come on then, this way. Let's make it official!"

"The orchid got returned thanks to the four of you," Tricia said. "You go on with Dr. Lukana. We'll be here when you're done."

Grandfather nodded. Even Anna Argent waved to them. So Henry, Jessie, Violet, and Benny followed Dr. Lukana down a narrow trail that went into the forest. The trail was canopied in tree leaves, loud with birds, and buzzing with bugs. Finally, Dr. Lukana stopped in a small grove where a big tree grew in the middle of a clearing. It was covered in thick moss, and in every nook and cranny of its bark were wild orchids of every color.

"Orange monkey orchids haven't been seen in Machu Picchu for fifty years," Dr. Lukana said. She set the glass case down and carefully removed the top so she could take the orchid out. "I prepared a special spot for this one when I heard from Tricia that she had found it."

Dr. Lukana lifted the orchid out of the case and gently placed it in the crook of one of the big tree's branches. She patted the roots down with moss. Right away, the orchid looked at home, shaded from the light by the tree's boughs and nourished by the rich, clean air of the mountains. The four Aldens gazed at it quietly until Benny exclaimed loudly, "We did it! We returned all the artifacts!"

His excitement made them all laugh.

"It feels great, doesn't it?" Henry asked.

"Do we have to go home right away? I want to look around Machu Picchu before we leave!" said Violet.

"Of course!" Jessie said. "Grandfather will be happy to look around with us too."

Benny took one last look at the orchid as they went back up the trail to where Grandfather, Tricia, and Anna waited. The wind blew through the orchid's leaves so it looked like it was waving. Benny waved back, then ran up the trail, looking forward to their next great adventure.

GERTRUDE CHANDLER WARNER discovered when she was teaching that many readers who like an exciting story could find no books that were both easy and fun to read. She decided to try to meet this need, and her first book, *The Boxcar Children*, quickly proved she had succeeded.

Miss Warner drew on her own experiences to write the mystery. As a child she spent hours watching trains go by on the tracks opposite her family home. She often dreamed about what it would be like to set up housekeeping in a caboose or freight car—the situation the Alden children find themselves in.

While the mystery element is central to each of Miss Warner's books, she never thought of them as strictly juvenile mysteries. She liked to stress the Aldens' independence and resourcefulness and their solid New England devotion to using up and making do. The Aldens go about most of their adventures with as little adult supervision as possible—something else that delights young readers.

Miss Warner lived in Putnam, Connecticut, until her death in 1979. During her lifetime, she received hundreds of letters from girls and boys telling her how much they liked her books.